Praise for Marilyn Levinson's
No Boys Allowed!

"Sensitive storytelling makes this story stand out."
— *Publishers Weekly*

"This is a timely book for young readers. . . . A touching story of a young girl working her way through an all too common heartbreak."
— *The Cryer*

". . . a sensitive portrayal of the feelings of a pre-adolescent girl as she struggles to understand her parents' divorce, her place in their lives, and her feelings about men."
— *Birmingham News*

MARILYN LEVINSON

Scholastic Inc.

New York Toronto London Auckland Sydney
Mexico City New Delhi Hong Kong Buenos Aires

No part of this publication may be reproduced, or stored in a retrieval
system, or transmitted in any form or by any means, electronic,
mechanical, photocopying, recording, or otherwise, without written
permission of the publisher. For information regarding permission,
write to Scholastic Inc., 557 Broadway, New York, NY 10012.

ISBN 0-439-71965-8

12 11 10 9 8 7 6 5 4 3 2   5 6 7 8 9 10/0

Printed in the U.S.A.   40

First Scholastic paperback printing, May 2005

For Bern. Stay in good health.

I was home when Daddy came for the rest of his stuff. It was a hot end-of-summer day, perfect for splashing around in my best friend Bobby Schaeffer's pool. Only I had this crazy urge to be here when Daddy picked up his CDs and his pipes and his golf clubs. And probably that dumb old stamp collection he'd brought from England when he was my age — eleven. The one he always talked about but never looked at, not in a hundred years.

This morning, when I told Mom I wanted to stay home, she said fine. She thought it would be a good idea for me to spend some time alone with Daddy, since he'd left it to her to tell me about the divorce. I didn't bother explaining that I had no intention of saying one word to him. It would only upset her. Right now she was across the street at Jessie's, probably crying her eyes out as she'd been doing these past two weeks — ever since Dad had dropped his bomb and moved out, all in the same evening. And Corinne? My fifteen-year-old sister was either at the beach or the mall, depending on whether her looks or her wardrobe needed more attention today.

Even though Daddy was supposed to be here at eleven, I was surprised when he pulled into the driveway right on the dot. How come he was on time as usual, when everything else about him had changed? I'd always considered my father, Colin Landauer, the most reliable, responsible person in the entire Western Hemisphere. But that was before he'd flipped out over the twenty-six-year-old lawyerette, as I used to call her, who came to work for his firm.

The second he cut the motor, I grabbed Tom, my cat, who'd been sunning himself on the plant table behind the living room couch, and raced to my room. I managed to shut myself inside before Daddy unlocked the front door.

"Corinne, Cassie," he called out. "Anyone home?" He knew that Mom wouldn't be here because she'd told him so on the phone yesterday. Right before I heard her tell him to leave the house keys on the kitchen table. I held my breath, wondering if he would walk down the hall to the bedrooms, but he didn't.

My room was stifling because it was ninety-two degrees out and the central air-conditioning wasn't working. It broke down a week ago, the day I came home from camp. Mom promised to get it fixed, but she never made the call. She always forgot to take care of things like calling repair people, but this time I couldn't blame her. She was still in shock over Dad's wanting a divorce so he could marry Corasue. Corasue. Now what kind of a name was that? It sounded more like a cartoon character than a person. A joke of a name, only I couldn't laugh.

The old fan that Mom had dug out of the basement was making a racket, so I couldn't hear what Daddy was doing.

Quietly, I opened my door and tiptoed down the hallway. Daddy was whistling as he collected books from the den and the living room and packed them into cartons. My temper blazed up at the sight of him acting so happy when the rest of us were miserable. After all, he wasn't just divorcing Mom, he was also moving far away — to Kentucky. He wouldn't be doing *that* if he really cared about Corinne and me, now would he?

I wanted to scream, as I usually did when I felt this angry, and to kick him in the shins. To stop him from being happy and let him know how bad he made me feel. Instead, I bit my lip and kept quiet. Most of all, I didn't want him to know I was watching him. But somehow he knew, because he stopped whistling and turned around.

"Cassie, are you there? Is that you, baby?"

I ran back to my bedroom and shut the door. I grabbed my desk chair and jammed it under the doorknob so he couldn't open the door.

"Cassie, let me in." My father was knocking.

No, you can't come in, I thought silently, furiously.

"Please open the door, honey. We're starting for Kentucky as soon as I've packed all my things here. I probably won't see you for a while."

And whose fault is that? I asked him in my mind. But it didn't occur to Daddy to think about *that*.

"Please, Cassie," Daddy pleaded. "I haven't seen you since Visiting Day at camp. I would have said something then, but nothing was definite. And what would have been accomplished if I did?" he asked with lawyerlike logic. "I would only have succeeded in ruining the rest of your stay at camp."

He knocked again, louder this time. "It's silly of you to behave like this. Like a little kid. You're not a baby anymore."

Who was he to tell me I was acting like a baby? I took a deep breath and almost started yelling, until I remembered my resolve never to speak to Daddy again.

"Well, I'm certainly not going to break down the door," Daddy said, half-joking, half-annoyed, "since your mother probably wouldn't get around to fixing it until sometime next winter."

How dare he make a crack about Mom! I picked up Tom and held him close until he yelped in pain. Then I threw myself down on my bed and cried and cried.

Tom woke me up by nuzzling my face — his way of letting me know he was hungry. I must have slept for hours, because the afternoon sun was streaming through the window. And Daddy's car was no longer in the driveway.

I found a note from Mom propped up on the kitchen table.

> Dear Cassie,
>   I came home at one and knocked on your door. When you didn't answer, I figured you wanted to sleep since you were up most of last night. I hope talking to your father didn't upset you too much. Jessie's taking me shopping. She thinks I should buy something crazy to help me feel better. I'll be home around five. See you then, sweetie.
>   I love you lots and lots, Mom

I fed Tom and made myself a tuna fish sandwich. I was finishing my lemonade when the phone rang. It was Bobby.

"Cassie! Where have you been?"

He sounded worried, and then I remembered. I'd told Bobby I'd come over for a swim just as soon as Daddy left.

"I've been here all the time. I guess I fell asleep."

"So that's why you didn't answer the phone," he said. "I thought maybe you went somewhere with your dad."

Bobby liked my father. Daddy appreciated that Bobby was a near genius in math and science, and could talk to Bobby about those things better than his own father could. They always — I mean, used to — kid around and tell each other the corniest jokes.

"He came by for his stuff, but I didn't talk to him."

Bobby was silent for a while. "Maybe you should have, Cassie. No matter what happened between him and your mother, he's still your father, right?"

For the first time in our six-year friendship, it bothered me that my best friend was a boy.

"Bobby," I said, forcing myself to be polite, "you just don't understand, okay?"

"He still loves *you*," Bobby persisted. "I know he does."

"Sure. That's why he's marrying Corasue and moving to Louisville just 'cause she's homesick. *Kentucky!*" I spit out the name of the state like it was a chicken bone. "Now who in his right mind leaves his family, his practice, and just about everyone he knows to go live in Kentucky?"

I was shouting by the time I finished making my point. Bobby was smart enough not to argue with me when I got this way.

"Come on over for a swim, Cassie. Kenny and his friends all left, so we can have the pool to ourselves without my brother hanging around."

I considered. The Schaeffers' Olympic-size pool was

tempting. It had a high, twisting slide and floats for drifting and gazing up at the sky. And even though he *was* a boy, Bobby was the kindest, most considerate friend in the whole wide world. I'd known that since the first day of kindergarten, when I'd come in crying and screaming that I wanted to go home and Bobby persuaded me to build a city of blocks with him instead.

But now wasn't the time for remembering. I suddenly knew what had to be done.

"I can't come over, Bobby. I have to take care of something around here."

"Okay, Cassie." He sounded disappointed. "See you later."

I found a carton in the garage and got to work, ridding the house of all traces of my father. If he didn't want to be here, good! Mom, Corinne, and I didn't need him. We didn't need *any* man. From now on, this would be a house for women only.

I decided to start in my parents' — I mean, my mother's — bedroom. I pulled open Daddy's bureau drawers. Empty. So was his closet, where he used to keep his three-piece lawyer suits in color-coordinated order. All that remained were a pair of jeans, a ratty old sweater, and an ugly tie hanging from the tie rack. "Out you go!" I shouted as I yanked all three loose and tossed them into the carton.

I threw out some toiletries I found in the bathroom. Next I checked the living room and the den. Daddy's pipe collection was gone. So were all his CDs, tapes, and computer stuff, as far as I could tell. I was disappointed. My father had done a thorough job of taking everything he wanted. Then I smiled as I remembered the basement.

Since our house was a ranch, our basement was pretty large. My parents had had most of it paneled and made into a playroom for Corinne and me when we were little. But there was a small room used for storage. It was full of folding chairs and pots and electric appliances that my parents didn't need any longer but didn't throw out because they were still in good shape. "We can always use this table or that coffeepot," they used to say, "when we buy our cottage at the shore." As long as I could remember, my parents had always talked about getting a cottage near the ocean. I almost started crying again as I pictured a little house facing the waves. Now we'd never have it. Never!

The room was a mess, with small pieces of furniture blocking the way to a large old bureau where my parents kept souvenirs from the past. Daddy's stamp album was in the very first drawer I opened. I recognized the fake leather cover at once. Inside, the loose-leaf pages were divided into little squares, the black-and-white pictures to show where the stamps were supposed to go. Daddy had put stamps on lots of the pages, but there were plenty of bare spaces, too.

Gleefully, I threw the album into the carton. There were photograph albums in the drawer also — of my parents' wedding and our family vacations. I reached for an album that looked older than the others. A shiver tingled down my spine as I leafed through photos of my father when he was still living in England. I slammed the book shut and threw it into the carton as well. It opened, and loose photographs spilled out. I gathered them into a pile and was about to rip them up, when I heard Mom's voice.

"Here you are, Cassie." She bent down to kiss my cheek. "I was wondering where you could be. What on earth are you doing?"

"Throwing out garbage."

Mom rummaged through the carton, then stretched out

her hand for the photos I was still holding. She looked at them and studied my face with her clear hazel eyes, trying to understand what was going on in my mind. Finally, she said, "Throw out the clothes and the stamp collection with my blessing. But do you really want to get rid of these photos?"

"Of course I do!" I exclaimed. "They're Daddy's. I don't want anything of his in this house."

Mom nodded. "Except they're also pictures of your grandma and grandpa. And here's an old picture of your great-uncle Harry. You really liked Uncle Harry the few times you saw him." She gathered up the photos and the photo album and put them back in the drawer.

"Now come on upstairs and see the beautiful dress Jessie made me buy. I kept telling her I had no use for it, but she insisted it was good for my morale."

"Sure, Mom. I'll be up in a minute. As soon as I finish going through these other drawers."

Mom sighed. Like Bobby, she knew when there was no point in arguing with me. "All right, Cassie. But don't start getting morbid about your father. No matter what I think of him, he's still your father. I'm glad you got to talk to him before he left for Kentucky."

I shook my head. "I wouldn't talk to him. Why should I?"

"Oh, Cassie." Mom took me into her arms.

Suddenly, the words I couldn't say all week came spilling from my mouth. "Why did he do it? Why did he leave us for *her*?" I hid my face in my mother's neck as tears gushed from my eyes. It felt good to cry, to let out all my feelings. Then I felt guilty because Mom started crying, too. We held on to each other and I thought: At least mothers don't leave you. Only fathers. Only men.

Mom blew her nose and wiped her eyes. She moved back

9

and perched on an old end table so she could look at me. I knew she was getting ready to give me an answer. Mom was forgetful and disorganized, but she never shrank from telling Corinne and me what she considered to be the facts of life.

"Who knows why he left, Cassie? I should have figured it out by now, since it's all I think about, morning and night." She gave a little laugh. "I must be dumb, but I never realized that your father had stopped loving me. I thought marriage meant commitment. Putting up with the other person's shortcomings."

Mom sighed. "I think deep down your father didn't see me as a serious person, partly because I never could get all excited about having a career. When I went back to college, he got upset every time I changed my major." She looked at me, a twinkle in her eye. "Although I have to admit, three majors in two years is a lot of majors. I guess it does seem kind of funny — a thirty-eight-year-old woman who can't decide what to do with the rest of her life."

I grabbed Mom and hugged her tight. "I don't care! Daddy's dumb to give you up." I patted the strawberry blond curls that framed her face. Even with red eyes and a runny nose, my mother was beautiful. And she had a good figure — compact and curvy in all the right places. "I bet you're prettier and sexier than *she* is, even if she's younger."

"According to Colin, Miss Corasue Williams is the ideal blend of beauty and brains," Mom said sarcastically, "with all the right priorities. She knows exactly what she wants, all right — a ready-made, live-in law partner."

She gave a little snort. "Well, I hope they argue plenty over who gets the biggest cases in bluegrass country. I'm betting on Corasue, since they're building their law practice on her family's wonderful connections. So far from the stress and *demands* of practicing in New York."

Mom got to her feet. "Now I'm going upstairs to put on that dress. I expect to see you in five minutes." She kissed me and I hugged her again. At least I had one parent whom I loved and could trust. Even if she was a little flaky.

I found a few more of Daddy's things and put them into the carton before going upstairs and dumping everything in one of the garbage cans in the garage. I was on my way to Mom's room when, for some crazy reason, I went back and retrieved the stamp album from the garbage. I left it on a shelf behind the cactus soil and planters. Then I went to find Mom.

She was in her bedroom twirling around in her new dress. "Do you like it?" she asked breathlessly. It was a gypsy dress — off the shoulder, with a dirndl bodice and a long, flowing skirt. The fabric was every color of the rainbow, all blending and chasing one another, but muted so that it was artistic instead of gaudy. Even I, who had no interest in clothes, could see why Jessie had insisted that my mother buy the dress. It looked as though someone had designed it especially for her.

"It's fantastic on you, Mom," I told her. "I'm glad you bought it."

Mom smiled. "So am I." She stroked the silky material of the skirt. "It was terribly expensive, but I got it on sale. Still, I feel kind of guilty since I can't imagine where I'll wear a dress like this." She gave a sad little laugh. "Colin would say I was being frivolous as usual. That I could just as easily have thrown my money down the garbage disposal."

I shook my head so hard, I felt dizzy. "Who cares what Daddy would say? He's not here, so it doesn't matter. It doesn't matter at all."

"I know, honey. It's a hard habit to break."

"Wow, what a way-out dress! Can I borrow it for Leslie's party Saturday night? Can I, Mom?" Corinne ran into the room and plopped herself down on Mom's bed.

My sister and I were both tall — like Dad — with long, dark hair, which Corinne spent a lot more time fussing with than I did. She had a gorgeous figure, too. As far as I was concerned, though, Corinne was beautiful on the outside only. Inside, she was selfish and self-centered. She didn't care much about school. Last year she'd squeaked by with a C average, which made Daddy very angry. But how much schoolwork could a person get done if she spent all her time talking on the phone and looking at herself in the mirror?

Still, that wasn't the *worst* thing about Corinne. The worst was that she didn't seem to care at all that Daddy had left us.

"It's Mom's dress, Corinne," I reminded her. "I think it would be nice if you let her wear it at least once before you grabbed it for yourself."

Corinne made a face, the same one she always made when I pointed out how selfish she was acting. I bet she never made that face to any of her friends, because her eyes bulged and her nose looked longer. Her witch face, I called it. It was how she really looked inside, *I* thought.

"Mind your own business, Cassandra. In fact, you'd better pay attention to your own clothes. You've been running around in the same shorts and polo shirt three days in a row. Ick!"

"Well, I have nothing else to wear," I blurted out, "and my trunk's not back from camp."

Mom put her hands to her head. "Oh, Cassie honey! I completely forgot. I'll do the laundry tonight."

That was Corinne, always starting trouble. As if Mom didn't have enough on her mind without worrying about laundry. Now she was busy examining Mom's dress. They both wore a size eight.

"What do you think, Mom?" Corinne's voice turned sweet, as if she hadn't just insulted me and made Mom sound like a negligent parent. "Do you think I could borrow it for the party? I promise to be careful and not get it dirty."

Mom sat on the bed and thought. Finally, she gave a little laugh. "Well, I can't see why not, especially since I probably won't have any occasion to wear it for a long, long time." She unzipped the back and stepped out of the dress. Faster than a bee could sting, Corinne had it folded over her arm. She put her other arm around Mom's shoulders.

"Thanks, Mom! You're an angel. I'll go and try it on with some high heels. Be back in a jiffy to show you how it looks."

"Why bother?" I said. "You're going to wear it no matter what Mom thinks."

Corinne flew out of the room, but first she stuck out her tongue at me. Naturally, I returned the gesture. What an awful sister she was! Too bad Daddy hadn't offered to take her to Kentucky with him and Corasue.

CHAPTER 3

Summer vacation ended and school began. I really didn't care either way. I'd always liked school, but now it was just a place to go. Although my teacher, Mrs. Morris, seemed nice enough, whatever she said sort of slipped from my mind as soon as she said it.

Today I found myself remembering some of our family traditions, and how I'd always taken our togetherness for granted. Like reading in my room on a rainy Sunday afternoon with Tom curled up beside me, knowing that Mom and Daddy and Corinne were doing different things in other rooms but were within shouting distance. The four Cs, Daddy used to call us: Colin, Claudia, Corinne, and Cassandra. The four C. Landauers of Shady Lane.

It suddenly hit me. I felt sick and raised my hand to be excused during Mrs. Morris's talk on the Egyptian gods and goddesses. Corasue began with a C as well.

Mr. Olson, our principal, spoke to us at our first assembly. "Your class is the last group of sixth graders to graduate from Harrison Elementary School. Starting next year, the sixth grade will be part of the Townsend Middle School. You are a very special group."

Mrs. Morris went on the stage, a big grin on her face, and talked about the upcoming events: putting together the first Harrison yearbook, the trip to Washington, D.C., the end-of-year play, and the graduation party. She ended by saying we should sign up for whatever committees we wanted to be on. As far as I was concerned, she was talking about signing up for a trip to the moon. It had nothing to do with me, Cassie Landauer.

But everyone else, it seemed, got all fired up about the end-of-school activities. Melissa and Janie — the two girls I ate lunch with — decided to work on the yearbook. Since they would often be using lunch hour for meetings, I decided I'd eat by myself.

Even Bobby, who hated anything organized like ball games, was all excited.

"Hey, Cassie, wait up!" he called after me when we got out at three o'clock.

I stopped and waited for him.

"Come on over to my house," Bobby said. "We have to decide what we want to work on."

"Work on?" I asked, puzzled.

"You know, which committee to join — for the graduation events. I think I'd like to do something with the play. Maybe paint scenery or work the lights."

I stared at him. "You've got to be kidding. Since when are you interested in joining committees?

"Where's your spirit, Cassie? We're graduating from Harrison. Moving on to the middle school. Don't you want to be a part of it all?"

"No, I don't want to be a part of anything," I snapped. "I have other things on my mind, more important things."

"I know you do," he said apologetically. "I was just trying to get your mind off of them."

There he was, being so *nice* when anyone else would have just snapped back at me. "I'll come over, Bobby, but only for a little while."

"Sure, Cass. And I promise not to twist your arm about signing up for something."

I wasn't very good company. Not for Bobby, not for anyone. Mom noticed I was acting like a zombie and gave me a pep talk about how I should remember that she loved me and that Daddy did, too.

She amazed me by proving to be stronger than I'd ever thought possible. She stopped crying and moping the same day Corinne and I went back to school. That very afternoon, when we were in the car on our way to buy school supplies, she turned to us and said, "Girls, I've decided not to go back to college. At least not until things settle down."

I shrugged, not at all surprised. I'd always thought that Mom had returned to school only because Daddy had wanted her to. I mean, how much could she have liked it if she couldn't make up her mind whether to become a teacher, a social worker, or an accountant? Mom was warm and wonderful but she was also scatterbrained. The truth was, she was happiest playing tennis and going out to lunch with Jessie and her other friends.

Now Mom was grinning. "I'm going to get a job."

The red light changed and Mom revved the motor. Corinne and I turned to each other, alarmed.

"Mom, you haven't worked since before I was born," Corinne said. "What will you do?"

"I'm not sure yet," she answered. "but I'll find something. Just you watch and see."

And sure enough, a few days later she actually had a job, working in Jessie's husband's friend's brand-new boutique in a shopping center not far from our house.

Daddy sent me letters, which I threw into the garbage unopened. He called every week to talk to Corinne and me, but I refused to get on the phone. Corinne acted like he was only away on a business trip. Whenever they talked, she giggled and told him about the cute boys in her classes and the parties she was invited to. I could have smacked her face for letting Daddy think that everything was fine, when he'd ruined all our lives.

Mom didn't speak to him when he called, either, because her lawyer had said not to. The divorce was moving along quickly. By October, it was supposed to be settled. Corinne reported that Daddy and Corasue were planning a small wedding in November. She and I were invited to visit the newlyweds during Christmas vacation. Ha! I told Corinne I'd rather be taken hostage and forced to eat mice than set foot in their house.

Shortly after Mom started her job in La Chique Boutique, we had another assembly in school. I tuned out when Mr. Olson introduced the speaker — a small, balding man — so at first I had no idea what he was gabbing about. Then I caught the word "stamps," then "stamp collection," and I started listening.

The speaker, Mr. Guerney, was saying that in spite of this being the age of computers and DVDs, lots of kids and adults collected stamps. He said it was fun and not very expensive — unless you bought a million-dollar stamp, ha-ha — and that the post office where he worked issued commemorative sheets from time to time, stamps printed to celebrate a special event or person. Lots of people who weren't even collectors saved them.

"Some collectors save only American stamps," Mr. Guerney went on. "Some prefer European stamps. There are those who pick a subject, like boats or flowers or sports, and collect only pictures of their subject. That's called topical collecting."

For the first time in weeks, I was willing to learn something new. Maybe I'd start collecting stamps from all over the world, the way Daddy did when he was a boy. Finally, Mr. Guerney asked if anyone had any questions. I was hoping someone would ask about collecting foreign stamps. No one did, and I considered raising my hand, but by then the assembly was over.

As soon as I got home from school, I took Daddy's stamp album from behind the planters and cactus soil in the garage. Tom followed me into my room. Even though we were alone in the house, I closed the door. I sat on my bed and leafed through the album. There was at least a page for every country. England and France and Denmark were pretty well filled in. So were Australia and Canada. Some of the other countries had pages only partly filled. Many countries didn't have one single stamp on their pages.

I closed the album and propped it under my chin while I thought. I wondered if there was any way I could finish

Daddy's old album. After I was done thinking, I slipped the album under my bed for safekeeping.

The next afternoon, I rode my bicycle into town, four blocks away. The post office was a small old building right off Main Street. I went inside and got in line. When it was my turn, I told the fat, gum-chewing postmistress that I wanted to speak to Mr. Guerney.

"Al-fieee," she shouted, embarrassing me to death. "There's another one here for you." She nodded, as if she'd just performed a good deed. "He'll be right with you."

Mr. Guerney came out from behind the counter, rubbing his hands and smiling. "Hello, hello. And what can I do for you, missy?

"My name is Cassandra Landauer, and I heard you speak at school yesterday," I said quickly. "About collecting stamps. I wanted to ask you something."

"Certainly, certainly." Now he was smiling so hard, I thought his face would split. "You're the fifth child to come as a result of my little talk. Are you interested in becoming a collector? We have the bird series in right now. Real beauties. Let me show them to you."

He was already turning to get them. I said loudly, "I don't want to see the birds."

A few people stared at me. There was nothing I hated more than being stared at in a public place. I could feel myself turning red. I spoke in a whisper.

"What I wanted to ask you, Mr. Guerney, is — can I still get stamps from years ago?"

"What did you say, Cassandra?" he asked. "Speak up. I can't hear you."

The same people looked at me. Now they were smiling, which was worse. I gritted my teeth and considered running out of the post office. But Mom would say I was letting my temper take over. I drew a deep breath and tried again. "I was wondering if I could possibly buy stamps that were printed years ago."

"Certainly, you can."

"Really?" I was surprised. "Stamps from all over the world?" I asked doubtfully.

"Why not?" He looked at me curiously. "But wouldn't you like to start by collecting American stamps? They're probably easier to get hold of."

"Well, I want to collect some American stamps," I said, remembering there were pages in the album for them, "but I have my father's album of international stamps and I want to finish it."

"Finish it?" He smiled broadly. "I don't know if anyone actually fills in every little space in any one album."

"Oh. I thought . . ." I wasn't sure what I thought.

"Now don't get discouraged before you've even begun. Once you start, you'll see how much you enjoy collecting stamps. They're beautiful little things, each one so different from any other. As you go along, you'll learn what's a good stamp and what you should avoid putting into your album."

Mr. Guerney leaned close to me, as if he were about to tell me a secret. "There's a store in Glen Haven, not twenty minutes from here. You can get a good start in one visit. Buy a packet of stamps for practically nothing, plus hinges and tongs for holding and mounting your stamps. The owner's a nice fellow. I buy plenty of foreign stamps there myself."

It sounded so nice and easy, but not for me. "Glen Haven's too far for me to ride on my bicycle," I complained.

Mr. Guerney waved his hand. "There you go, getting discouraged again. You'll just have to make use of the good old U.S. Postal Service and write away for your stamps. Now let me see if I can remember the exact address."

He scratched his chin, then wrote on a pad. He ripped off the page and handed it to me. "Just write to this company and tell them you want a packet of two hundred foreign stamps." He told me the price, which wasn't very expensive at all.

"Hey, this is great!" I was feeling hopeful again.

"Later on, you'll probably want to buy packets from different countries. They cost a bit more." He looked at me curiously. "How old is your album?"

I told him the date Daddy had written on the flyleaf.

"Ah," Mr. Guerney said thoughtfully. "If your album is loose-leaf, you may want to add pages for the countries that have been created since then."

"And some countries have changed names," I said, suddenly seeing my project double in size. "Well, thanks a lot. I'll send for the stamps tonight."

Then he smiled. "Bring in your album one day. I'd be happy to look at it."

"Sure, Mr. Guerney. I'll do that." I offered him my hand and we shook on it.

CHAPTER 4

I rode home thinking about what Mr. Guerney had told me. I could get a packet of stamps as he had suggested. But if I ordered stamps through the mail, Mom and Corinne might see them and wonder why I wanted them. I mean, it wasn't actually a *secret* that I was going to finish Daddy's stamp album. I just didn't want anyone to know.

The closer I got to our house, the less I wanted to have to explain about the album. Mom thought I had thrown it out with the trash. I wanted to leave it at that.

So, instead of turning onto Shady Lane, I went two blocks farther to Sunset, where Bobby lived.

"Hi, Cassie!" he said, opening the door for me. "Come into the kitchen. Mom went food shopping last night. We have those chocolate chip cookies you like."

"Great, because I'm starving. I was in such a rush to get to the post office, I forgot to have a snack."

I followed him into the Schaeffers' kitchen, which was almost as familiar to me as my own. He filled a glass with chocolate milk and put the cookie jar on the table.

Bobby waited patiently while I drank my milk and ate two cookies before he asked, "Why did you go to the post office, Cass? Were you sending something off to your dad?"

"I certainly was not!" I wiped off my brown mustache with a napkin. "I went to see Mr. Guerney. I'm thinking of starting a stamp collection."

"You? Collecting stamps? Cassie, you've never collected anything in your life."

I sighed. Bobby knew me too well. I was going to have to tell him more than I wanted to. "Well, I came across this stamp album my father had when he was about our age — and at that assembly, I got the idea to fill it in."

Bobby nodded slowly. "That's a good idea, Cassie. It will give you something to share with your father even though he's not around."

"That's *not* why I'm doing it. I thought collecting stamps might be fun, but" — I made the story up as I went along — "my mom might get upset if she knew I was using Dad's old album — she's so angry with him. So I was wondering if, when I order stamps, I could have them sent here instead of to my house."

I closed my mouth and waited. Most of what I'd said was true, with a slight twist of the facts. I needed his help, and I was only putting it in a way that I thought he'd understand.

"Sure, Cassie. You can have whatever you want sent here." He paused, but he wasn't finished. When he went on, he looked down at the table instead of at me. "It just sounds kind of weird, that's all."

"It sounds weird?" I shouted guiltily. "Why is that? Is it so weird that my mom is upset because my father left her for a younger woman? I mean, he turned our lives upside down."

Bobby poured me another glass of chocolate milk. "Look,

Cassie, I said you could send the stamps here. And I'm sorry about your mother. Divorce is pretty awful. But ever since your father left, it seems you're always angry at me. No matter what I say, you jump down my throat. You know, I don't like it that your father went away, either. I miss talking to him."

A lump filled my throat, and I could feel tears starting in my eyes. But I wouldn't break down. Not over my father. Not here, in front of Bobby.

"Well, I don't miss him one bit! Mom, Corinne, and I are getting along just fine."

"If you're getting along so well," Bobby answered, "I wish you'd stop yelling all the time and acting like it's my fault."

I stared at him in disbelief. "You're some friend, Bobby Schaeffer! You really don't understand what I'm going through. All you think about is yourself. You're as selfish as Corinne."

I got up. "And I don't need your charity. I'll find another way of getting the stamps, don't you worry."

Before he could answer, I was through the front door and heading for home.

I sent away for the stamps that very night. As I licked the flap of my envelope, it dawned on me that I could have avoided that whole ugly scene with Bobby if I'd only thought things out more. I always got home before Mom and Corinne, which meant I didn't have to worry about their finding the stamp packet in the mail, after all. Mom, who didn't like her job as much as she had at first, didn't get back till dinnertime. And Corinne was always staying after school to watch the boys' soccer practice or some such activity.

Everything my sister did now had something to do with boys. Ick! A few times, I overheard her talking to her girlfriends on the phone about someone named Jason. And she was wearing more makeup than she used to — tons of eye shadow and liner and mascara.

"Where are you going, all painted like that?" I asked her one morning. "To an audition for *Bride of Frankenstein?*" Corinne stormed out the door without finishing her breakfast. Wow, was she touchy!

The packet arrived two weeks later, on a Thursday. I opened it up and was dazzled by the sight of so many stamps. They were all different colors and sizes. I tried to sort them according to country, but I realized I'd need lots of envelopes and several hours to do the job. Tomorrow I'd buy hinges and tongs for mounting the stamps, at the hobby store in town.

The stamps were all canceled, which meant they had traveled, many of them halfway across the world, on letters and packages. I examined a few of them, trying to figure out if they were in good condition or not. I had no way of knowing, since I didn't know what I was supposed to look for. I could find out by getting books on stamp collecting from the library. I felt a thrill of excitement as I ran my hands through the stamps. Suddenly, I had so much to do and not enough time to do it.

I slipped the packet of stamps under my bed at last and started working on a report for school. Corinne came home and stuck her head into my room. "That was some soccer game," she said, like I was really interested. "And that Jason

Braverman is the very best center. He scores more goals than anyone else on the team."

I sighed. "Corinne, I have to work on my report."

"Oh, your report." She went into her room and slammed the door. Soon hard rock was shaking the wall between our rooms.

I ran into Corinne's room. She was actually at her desk with a book opened. "Turn that down!" I shouted. "I can't hear myself think."

Corinne shook her head. "If I can study with it, so can you."

I yelled at her again, but she ignored me. Since I couldn't get any more work done, I went into the den to watch TV.

Mom arrived a few minutes later with a barbecued chicken for our dinner. I started setting the table, since it was my turn that week.

"Hi, honey." Mom gave me a hug and a kiss. "How's school?"

I made a face. "Boring. How's work?"

Mom sighed. "Work is awful. I think I'm going to quit."

"You're what?"

Mom picked up on the fear in my voice and laughed.

"Don't worry, Cassie. We won't starve. The job isn't for me, that's all. I'm no good at catering to all those wealthy women. They have about as many outfits in their closets as we carry in the boutique. And I'm supposed to tell them how great they look, when they look like clowns because the styles are for kids Corinne's age."

"Mom," I gasped. "It's your job. You're supposed to tell them they look nice. Even I know that."

Mom shook her head. "Well, I can't and I won't. There are

plenty more jobs to be had in this world. Tomorrow I'm giving Don two weeks' notice."

I had a sudden thought. "Maybe you should go back to college next semester and find a career you really like."

Mom reached over and brushed the hair off my forehead. "No, I won't, Cassie. You'll go to college and become a doctor or a lawyer or whatever you choose to be. I'll find a job that I like."

"But, Mom —"

"There are no buts about it," Mom said firmly. "I make the decisions about my life now."

I nodded, seeing she was right.

"Is Corinne home?" she asked, sounding more like herself.

"She's in her room studying."

"I'm happy to hear that. Please tell her we're eating in five minutes."

CHAPTER 5

True to her word, Mom found another job — with a small theater company that had its office in an old, dilapidated barn out in the country. Not that Mom spent much time in the office. RBP — short for Red Barn Players — put on plays all over the area. Mom's job was to help out wherever she was needed. She typed up playbills, got the tickets from the printer, painted scenery, and sewed costumes. By the second week, she was even working the lights. She loved every minute of it.

"The job's terrific, Cassie," she told me when we went to deposit her first paycheck in the bank. "It's fun, it's exciting. And the best thing is, I don't do the same thing every day." She laughed, her old happy laugh from the time before Daddy left us. "Of course they don't pay all that much, and I wish I didn't have to work so many evenings. But" — Mom waved her hand dramatically — "as Jeff says, that's show biz."

Jeff was codirector of RBP when he wasn't busy teaching English at a nearby high school. According to Mom, Jeff was kind and funny and talented. He was divorced from Nancy, the group's other codirector. "It's a friendly divorce," Mom explained. "They squabble a lot, but deep down I think they still love each other."

I sure was glad to hear that. Lately, Mom managed to bring Jeff's name into every conversation. I knew she wouldn't listen to *me*, but the last thing she needed right now was a boyfriend.

Bobby and I made up, and he called one day and invited me to come over.

"I can't," I told him. "I have to put all these stamps in order before I can mount them in the album. Then I have a ton of library books about stamps to read, and I want to stop at the post office to look at the collectors' sheets Mr. Guerney told me about."

Bobby sighed. "I don't know, Cassie. It sounds like you're letting this stamp business take over your life."

"It keeps me busy," I agreed. "I hardly even have time to do my homework."

"Cassie!" Bobby was shocked. "You're not letting your math slip, are you?" he asked, knowing math was my one downfall. "Want me to come over and go over the stuff with you?"

"No, thanks," I said, though I could have used his help. We were having a math test at the end of the week, but I didn't have time for any tutoring session. "Listen, I have to go. See you in school."

I went back to my room, my thoughts on the stamps waiting for my attention. I wondered what Daddy would say if he could see me working on his old album. Probably not much, since he'd forgotten about it just as he'd forgotten about me.

I wanted to buy more stamps for my album, but I wasn't sure what was available. I needed to visit that store in Glen Haven. But I still hadn't figured out how to get there.

*   *   *

I failed the math test. If this had happened before Daddy left us, I would have died of shame. But when I saw the red 57 on my paper, I only shrugged and told myself it wasn't important.

On Monday, Mrs. Morris asked me to stay when everyone else went to lunch.

"Cassie," she said as soon as we were alone, "I want to talk to you about your schoolwork."

I figured I'd play it smart by saying what she was about to and get it over with. "I know. I failed the math test on Friday. I'll study more next time. It won't happen again."

Mrs. Morris smiled, but she looked sad. "It's not just the test. You don't pay attention to what's going on in the classroom. It's only because you are so intelligent that you haven't failed a test before this."

I bit my lip, wondering what to say. Mrs. Morris went on.

"I understand that things have been rough at home, with your parents' sudden separation and your father going so far away. But if you don't start paying attention in class and doing your homework, I'm going to have to call your mother."

"Please don't call her," I said quickly. "Mom's busy with her new job and she doesn't need to worry about me." I took a deep breath. "I'll try to concentrate more in class."

"And do your homework?"

"And do my homework."

Mrs. Morris nodded. "All right, then. Let's see how it goes."

After that, I made a real effort to listen in class. The more I paid attention, the easier it got. And I asked Bobby to tutor me in math once a week. Soon I was raising my hand and giving answers. I started eating lunch with Melissa and Janie again. Once I overheard Mrs. Morris telling another sixth-grade teacher that I was "adjusting to my situation."

Let her think that, I thought. That's how much *she* knows about me.

One evening in early November, Mom called Corinne and me into the den.

"Girls," she began, "the divorce has gone through." Mom's eyes were glittering, and I couldn't tell if she was happy or angry. "Your mother is now a free woman."

Corinne and I saw that Mom was trying to be brave, so we hugged her and offered our congratulations.

"All I can say is, I'm happy it's over. You'll be spending summers and long vacations with Daddy."

"Not me." I made a face.

"Cassie, we'll talk about that later. What I want to say is, money's very tight. From now on, we have to watch every penny we spend." Mom looked at Corinne. "That means no new outfits until spring."

"But, Mom," Corinne complained, "you said I could buy something for the freshman dance. Everyone's seen all my clothes at least ten times."

"Well, maybe a new top, but that's it. And I'm going to have to cut down on the take-out foods. Corinne and Cassie, you're going to start helping prepare dinner. It's much cheaper that way."

"Why, Mom?" I asked. "Daddy makes lots of money."

Mom pursed her lips. When she spoke, her voice was bitter. "Your father *made* lots of money, but he's not making it right now. And he's claiming heavy financial losses because of that foolish move of his. He and his shrewd lawyer have managed to present a solid case for giving us much less than what he'd promised me in August."

"Do we have to sell the house?" Corinne asked.

"I think we can manage — if we're careful," Mom said.

Now I was really scared. I'd never thought much about money before, since we'd always had enough for anything we wanted.

"Maybe I could get a job delivering newspapers, Mom," I said.

"Cassie, that's very sweet of you, but you'd have to get up early Sunday mornings and go out in bad weather. With my job having such irregular hours, I won't always be home to help you."

"That's all right," I said. The more I thought about having a paper route, the more I liked it. I would be helping out. Besides, I'd have money to buy new stamps. "Can I keep some of the money I make?" I asked.

Mom got up and hugged me. "Honey, of course you can. We're not going to be as poor as you're making it sound. We'll be fine as long as we're careful."

All this time, Corinne seemed to be studying Mom. Finally, she asked, "Mom, don't you think that maybe you should try to get a job that pays more money?"

"No, Corinne," Mom snapped. "I'm not going to give up the one thing I enjoy. We'll manage if we all do our part."

I stroked Tom, who sat purring beside me, not knowing or caring that now we had money problems on top of everything else. I promised myself I'd never speak to another male person ever again, unless I absolutely had to. Except for Bobby, who was still my best friend. And Tom, who didn't count because he was a cat.

I walked around in a fog the next few days. Mom and Daddy were actually divorced! I suppose deep down, in the most secret corner of my heart, I'd been hoping that Daddy would come home and say it was all a mistake. That he realized he couldn't live without us. Maybe I should have called at least once to ask him if he'd change his mind.

Corinne spoke to Daddy that week as usual. When she got off the phone, she was grinning.

"Guess what? Daddy and Corasue are getting married on Thanksgiving Day. He wishes we could be there, but would rather have us come at Christmas when we can spend more time together."

"Who cares what he wants?" I shouted.

"Well, I wish I could go to the wedding," she said softly, "and meet Corasue. She's going to be our stepmother, whether you like it or not."

I stared at Corinne in disbelief. "How can you even say such a thing? I'm glad Mom isn't home to hear you turn traitor."

"I'm not a traitor, but I refuse to give up Daddy the way you have."

"Give *him* up? Corinne, he gave *us* up. Why don't you admit he's selfish and irresponsible? He's not even giving us enough money to live on."

Corinne glared at me. "How do you know all this? You haven't spoken to him since Visiting Day at camp. He's doing the very best he can."

"Only his best isn't good enough, is it? Face it, Corinne, we don't matter very much to Daddy anymore." But Corinne didn't hear me. She'd stormed back to her room and set her music blasting.

CHAPTER 6

T he following week, I got a job delivering newspapers. Luckily, my route was close to our house
and included Bobby's street. Sometimes I'd drop
off the Schaeffers' paper and find Bobby waiting to help me
with the rest of my route.

"You don't have to," I told him.

"I know," he said, grinning, "but I figured you could use
the company."

In spite of the cold and rainy November weather, I appreciated having my paper route. It helped fill up my week-
ends and the long afternoons. Mom and Corinne were
hardly ever around, and I felt lonely at home, even with
Tom to keep me company. Besides, the house itself was different. It was turning into a mess.

Mom was one of the world's worst housekeepers, and
now that she was spending more and more hours with the
theater group, the house was getting dirtier and messier.
One evening, Mom asked Corinne to vacuum and dust.
Corinne said okay, but she never got around to doing it. Finally, she and Mom got into an argument.

"Why can't Cassie do some of the cleaning?" Corinne asked.

"Because she's doing her share with the paper route. Besides, she feeds Tom and changes his kitty litter."

"Well, she should," Corinne said. "He's her mangy pet, nobody else's."

Mom sighed and said she'd do it herself. But she was always too busy or too tired to do more than sweep crumbs off the kitchen floor.

On Friday morning — a week after Thanksgiving and Daddy's wedding — the bathroom was so disgustingly grimy that I decided to clean it when I got back from my paper route. I was surprised when I came home later that afternoon and found Mom scrubbing the bathtub and singing at the top of her voice.

"You're cleaning!" I said.

"I sure am," Mom said, sounding happier than someone scrubbing a bathtub ordinarily sounded. "We have no performances this week, so Jeff gave me a three-day vacation. With pay." Then she grinned. "It's about time I took this house in hand, don't you think? I mean, what would people say if they walked in and saw such a dirty mess?"

I shrugged. Hardly anyone besides our neighbor Jessie ever came in anymore. "Can I help, Mom?"

"Sure, honey. Get a rag in the closet and the dust spray under the kitchen sink and start on the living room furniture."

"Okay." I got to work and started singing along with Mom. It felt good, putting the house back into shape.

Corinne came home, and Mom got her to vacuum without putting up a squawk. I finished the living room and the dining room, then dusted the bedrooms. Two hours later, the house was sparkling and bright.

Mom walked into the den, where Corinne and I were putting the finishing touches on the bookcase. She put her arms around us. "Girls, we did a magnificent job. I think we deserve a reward, so I'm taking us out to dinner."

We went to the local diner, just as we used to on Friday nights. For the first time in months, I felt I was part of a family. The three of us acted silly, and we laughed a lot. Mom told Corinne and me funny stories about the people in RBP. The best was about one actor's pants falling down right in the middle of a performance and how he'd managed to hold them up so the audience never noticed. Then Corinne had to ruin everything by talking about Jason Braverman.

"I really think he likes me, Mom," she said, going all soppy. "He always stops to talk to me after third period. And he told Leslie's brother that I'm the prettiest girl in class." Corinne gave a deep sigh. "Leslie just found out he's coming to the party tomorrow night."

Mom winked. "It sounds like he's interested, all right."

"Do you really think so?"

I couldn't believe how *pathetic* my sister sounded. She was ruining our fun evening with her mushy conversation.

"How boring can you get, Corinne?" I said. "All you talk about is this Jason. This *boy*."

"Just wait and see, Cassie," Mom said, smiling. "You won't be very different in a couple of years."

"Not me," I corrected Mom. Not in a million years, I added, but I didn't say it out loud.

The next day, Saturday, Mom and Corinne went shopping at the mall. I stayed home and worked on my stamp album. It was fun, matching up the right stamp with the right square, then putting a little hinge on the stamp and setting it in its place. I had no trouble finding the less expensive stamps, but there weren't too many of larger denominations in the packet. I could see they were harder to come by, especially since Daddy's book was so old. But I wasn't discouraged. I could look for those stamps in a stamp store or order them through a catalog.

I was up to the M's — Mexico, Monaco. Every time I started a new country, I looked it up on the map and read about it in the *World Almanac.* Maybe, when I was older, I could visit some of these countries. I could get a job as a journalist or something that would take me to foreign places. I'd learn different languages and see wondrous things. Maybe I'd ride a camel or go on a safari in Africa. I could travel from place to place and never be tied down. Not by a husband or children or anyone.

Mom and Corinne came home around four-thirty, loaded with packages. They chattered happily and showed me what they'd bought. "Here, honey." Mom handed me a hunter green shirt. "This is for you."

"Oh, Mom," I groaned. "I told you I didn't need anything."

"Try it on, try it on," she ordered, laughing.

I slipped it over my turtleneck and looked at my reflection in the mirror. "I like it," I had to admit.

"Good, because I picked it out," Corinne said. And before I could come up with some wisecrack, she went on.

"Just wait till you see the new top I got. You'll really flip." Just because I liked the shirt, she was acting as if I'd suddenly become as clothes-crazy as she was. "Actually, I bought it for the dance next week, but I'm going to wear it tonight so Jason can see it. I'll go try it on with my good jeans."

Corinne went to her room. Mom took some nuts and candy from another package and started filling candy dishes.

"Why are you putting out candy and stuff?" I asked, watching her set them on the coffee table in the living room. "Are we having company?"

Mom smiled. "Jeff's stopping by after dinner. We thought we'd take in a movie, then come back here for a while."

"You're going out with *Jeff*? On a *date*?"

Mom gave a little laugh. She sounded nervous. "Not a date, exactly. Just two friends who've decided to spend a free evening together."

Suddenly, I understood why she'd been so happy yesterday and today. "So that's why you finally cleaned the house," I shouted. "You didn't care that it was disgusting for Corinne and me. It only matters for Jeff."

"Cassie, yesterday I was free. It was the perfect day to tackle the cleaning. You're getting upset over nothing."

"I'm *not* upset," I said. "I only wish you could have told me about your date instead of springing it on me. Like you did the divorce."

"Now, Cassie, that isn't fair," Mom was saying as I grabbed my jacket and ran out of the house.

It was cold and windy outside. I wished I'd thought to bring my hat and gloves. I hated walking around in the dark, but I didn't want to be in my house, either. Nothing was right anymore. No one knew what I was feeling. No one had ever really understood me. Except Daddy. So many times he'd come into my room to ask me why I was sad or upset or angry about something. And we'd talk, and finally he'd make a dumb joke and get me to smile.

Tears streamed down my face, and I rubbed them away with my fists. I didn't want to remember Daddy being nice. Or the fact that he understood me better than anyone else in the whole wide world.

I was so upset, I didn't pay any attention to where I was walking. When I calmed down, I found myself standing in front of Bobby's house. Lights shone from every window, making it look warm and inviting. I rang the bell. Kenny, Bobby's older brother, opened the door.

"Hi, Cassie." Without waiting for me to answer, he turned around and shouted, "Cassie's here, Bobby. And hurry up. Dad says we're leaving for the hockey game in ten minutes."

Kenny disappeared, and I stepped into the hall. In a minute, Bobby came bounding down the steps.

"Hi, Cass, what's up?" he asked.

"My mom has a date," I told him, gulping air. "She's going to the movies with Jeff."

"So what's wrong? I thought you said he's been really nice to her."

"Bobby, she's been divorced hardly a month."

Bobby smiled. "Oh, Cassie, give her a break. Your mom's entitled to have some fun once in a while. She's only going to the movies."

A sudden rage came over me. How dare he tell me it was no big deal that my mother was going out with Jeff? How would he like it if *his* father were dating instead of taking Kenny and him to a hockey game?

I swung open the front door. "You don't understand,

Bobby Schaeffer!" I shouted over my shoulder. "You don't understand at all!"

Dinner was miserable. Mom tried to talk to me, but I wouldn't respond to anything she said. I twirled my spaghetti and hardly put any in my mouth. Finally, I dumped it into the garbage and went to my room. I threw myself onto my bed. My mind was as empty as the darkened room. I felt exhausted. Worn out. All I wanted to do was sleep.

A few minutes later, someone knocked and turned on a light. Blinking, I turned around, expecting to see Mom. It was Corinne.

"You really hurt Mom's feelings, behaving in that obnoxious way," Corinne informed me, speaking as if she were twenty years old. "She has a perfect right to go to the movies with Jeff if she wants."

"Then let her go," I mumbled into my pillow. "Just remember, Jeff's a man, so he'll probably hurt her. And she'll be more miserable than ever."

Corinne shook my arm. "Come on, Cassie. Don't do this to Mom. You're acting like all men are bad news."

"They are. Each and every one of them," I said.

Corinne laughed as if I'd made a joke.

CHAPTER 7

Corinne finished her big-sister lecture and left. Soon after, she and Mom started primping for their evening out. They kept running into each other's room, asking how this looked and that matched. Corinne borrowed Mom's gold bracelet. Mom borrowed Corinne's mascara. And all the while, Corinne didn't shut up about Jason. It was nauseating.

How could they fuss so much for the sake of some male? How could they have forgotten what Daddy had done to us? If he could stop caring, well, then any man could. We women had to stick together. We had to be strong. A plan formed in my head.

The moment Corinne and Mom left, I scrounged around in the garage until I found exactly what I wanted: a piece of paneling two feet long. I brought it into the kitchen and got my colored markers. The paneling was a light color, left over from when we redid the den two years ago. Purple would stand out.

I wrote WOMEN ONLY in big block letters. And, to make

my message even clearer, I added NO MEN ALLOWED in the space below. Pleased with my artwork, I hung the sign from the knocker on the front door, then ran shivering down the walk to get a better view. The sign looked great. It was impossible to miss! Grinning, I made a mug of hot chocolate and helped myself to some of the candy in the living room.

I couldn't have hoped for a better reaction. My sign was the very thing Mom and Jeff were discussing as they returned from the movies. I'd left my bedroom door wide open so I wouldn't miss one word.

"I can't believe Cassie actually made a sign like that," I heard Mom say. "She's never done anything like this before. I'm sorry, Jeff. And terribly embarrassed."

"Don't be, Claudia." Jeff had a deep voice. "From what you've told me, Cassie sounds like a bright and sensitive girl. She feels she's been abandoned by her father, so she's taking it out on every man who crosses her path."

I was about to give Jeff full points for compliments and accuracy when he let out a knowing laugh. Then I knew he was only showing off. "My daughter reacted badly when Nancy and I split. And I moved only four blocks away."

"I'm worried," Mom said. "Cassie refuses to visit Colin over the Christmas vacation. She hasn't spoken to him since I told her about the divorce. And that was almost four months ago."

"Maybe I'd better leave so you can talk to her."

I almost clapped when Mom didn't try to stop him from going. Jeff left and Mom stormed into my room, my sign in her hand.

"How could you do such a thing, Cassandra?" she demanded. "It was rude to me and hostile toward Jeff."

"Well, I don't want any man coming into our house. We don't need them."

"We don't need them?" Mom hit her head with her hand. "As usual, you're letting your angry feelings take over. Just remember, *you* don't decide who comes into this house."

"We have to be strong, Mom, and show that we don't need men. We can manage fine without them."

Mom looked at me for a while. I was sitting at my desk and she crouched next to me. "Honey, you're developing a terrible attitude toward men because of what happened with Daddy. Not every man would do what Daddy did if he found himself attracted to a young colleague."

"But we don't *need* any men around here," I insisted again.

Mom smiled. "Yes, we do. For fun. For companionship. For romance."

"Ick," I said. I didn't want to talk about it anymore. "Mom, since Jeff's gone, do you think I could finish off the candy?"

Mom thought about it. "As long as you promise not to put that sign up ever again."

"I'll leave it on my bedroom door," I said.

"Fair enough," Mom agreed, and we shook on it.

I was just drifting off to sleep when Corinne came home. She started shrieking and jumping all over the house.

"He likes me! Jason likes me! We're going to the movies tomorrow afternoon with some other kids. I'm so happy, I could die."

I walked out of my bedroom rubbing my eyes. "Thanks for waking me up, Miss Consideration."

"Oh, Cassie," Corinne pooh-poohed me. "This is more important than sleep. Wait till you meet Jason. Even a man hater like you will have to agree that he's gorgeous."

Was that what I was? A man hater? It didn't sound very nice.

It snowed the following Wednesday, and school was closed — our first snow day. After the flurries stopped around three o'clock, Jason came by and shoveled our walk and driveway. I suppose most girls would say he was good-looking — at least, those who went for the dark, curly-haired type with a great smile and soulful eyes. And he had good manners. Mom tried to pay him for shoveling, but he blushed and refused to take any money.

"It's all right, Mrs. Landauer. I was glad to do it." Then he and Corinne went into the den and watched TV. When I happened to walk by, they were giggling and tickling each other. I bet they didn't get to see much of the movie they had blasting away. I felt like taking my sign and putting it in front of the TV, but that would only have made Mom and Corinne angry. Anyway, it looked like it would take more than a sign to get rid of Jason Braverman.

Thursday, Bobby was waiting for me when I dropped off his family's newspaper. We sat down on the front steps of his house.

"I'm sorry I yelled at you Saturday night," I said. "I was upset."

"Forget it. How did your mom's date with Jeff go?"

I told him about the sign I'd put up and how successful it had been. "Mom and Corinne are worried that I'm turning into a man hater."

"Are you?" Bobby asked.

"Why shouldn't I?" I replied defensively. "We trusted Daddy and he deserted us. If he can do that, any man can."

Bobby stood up. "Well, I'm going to be a man one day, and I don't ever intend to leave my wife and children — when I have them, that is."

The thought of Bobby with a wife and children made me laugh. I stood up and rubbed my hands together. "I better deliver the rest of these papers. Want to come?"

"Can't," Bobby said. "I have lots of math homework to do. Which reminds me, you have that big test next week. Want me to help you review?"

"Ick," I said, remembering. "How's next Tuesday afternoon? At my house."

"Okay." Bobby turned to go into his house. "See you in school."

Christmas vacation was ten days away. When Mom wasn't around, Corinne talked about how she couldn't wait to see Daddy, and how she was going to miss Jason. It was getting on my nerves.

"If you're so worried about missing Jason," I told her, "don't go to Louisville. Stay home with me."

"You know you're going to have to come with me in the end, Cassie," she said.

"Absolutely not," I said. "Mom didn't say I had to go, either."

"Well, Daddy will get a court order," Corinne said, "and you'll have to go."

"Nobody can make me," I answered back, but I was nervous. A court order? Would Daddy really do that?

I didn't want to ask Mom about it because lately she hadn't been acting like herself. She was irritable and snapped at Corinne and me for the littlest thing. Deep down, I was sure it was my fault for ruining her date with

Jeff. Still, maybe she was unhappy because the vacation was coming up. We'd always gone away during the holidays, but this year there wasn't enough money for Mom and me to go anywhere.

Saturday morning, Mom and I were eating breakfast when we heard the mailman. Mom jumped up to get the mail. She leafed through everything until she got to a large manila envelope.

"Ah, here it is! A week late but —" She ripped open the envelope. There were two plane tickets, a note, and a check. Mom glanced at the note and threw it on the table. She stared at the check as if she couldn't believe what she saw. Then she stamped her foot. "Oh, no, you don't, Colin! You're not going to get away with this!"

"What is it, Mom?" I asked. "What's wrong?"

"Not only did your father send the monthly check ten days late, but he's chiseled it down to nothing. He wrote me a note complaining about his money problems and some other tale of woe. Like I'm supposed to care. Well, I don't. And what's more, I refuse to be stepped on any longer."

"What are you going to do?" I asked, almost afraid to find out.

"Call him — that's what."

CHAPTER 8

Mom took her address book from the kitchen desk drawer and started punching in numbers. Her hand shook so much, she made a mistake and had to begin again. "There!" she said, and tapped her fingers until someone answered. Daddy barely had time to say hello before Mom ripped into him.

"Colin, I signed an agreement for far less money than was good for me and the girls, and now you're not even sending us *that*. I want the full amount, not installments."

Daddy said something that made Mom even angrier.

"I don't want to hear about your problems. Save it for Corasue. I need the money for basics, like paying the mortgage and buying groceries."

Dad said something else, which Mom quickly interrupted. "No! I will *not* take it from the little savings I have. You mail it out or I'll have your assets frozen."

"Rah, rah," I whispered, punching the air like a cheerleader. Mom was terrific! I'd never heard her speak like that before. It seemed Daddy hadn't, either.

"Too bad if you've never seen this side of me," Mom was

saying. "You did a very good job of bringing it out, though, didn't you — dropping us and choosing to live out your fantasy. Well, reality's set in, Colin, and now you're paying for it."

Mom listened. Her lips tightened into a frown. "Yes, the tickets came. And no, Cassie hasn't changed her mind."

I held my breath while Daddy talked about me, wondering if he could make me go there. But I didn't have to worry. Mom supported me all the way.

"Colin, don't threaten me with your lawyer jargon. It doesn't work anymore. If Cassie doesn't want to see you, I won't put her on that plane. And make sure the rest of our monthly check is in the mail today, or I'll reopen proceedings and ask for more alimony *and* more child support."

I clapped and cheered, not caring if Daddy heard me. Mom was magnificent. It sounded like Daddy was impressed, too, because Mom smiled as she said, "Thanks for the compliment, but I have no intention of becoming a lawyer. I'm happy being what I am. Just send me the right amount every month, that's all I'm asking."

She paused as Daddy changed the subject, and her expression softened. "So you've heard from Uncle Harry. It's been quite some time." Daddy talked a bit more, and Mom said, "I'm sorry to hear that. I'll give him a call."

Mom hung up the receiver and I grabbed her. "I'm so proud of you, Mom. You sure told him off."

She grinned. "I must admit, it felt good to put your father in his place. But the true measure of my success will be whether or not he sends us the money." Then she shrugged. "I refuse to worry about it. If I don't get that check by Friday, I'll call my lawyer and let him handle it."

"What did Daddy say about Uncle Harry?"

"It seems Uncle Harry called your father in Louisville.

Uncle Harry had a heart attack and he's home recuperating, with nurses around the clock." Mom shook her head and sighed. "Poor Uncle Harry. We didn't even know he was sick." She paged through her address book. "I think I'll call him right now."

"And I think I'll go and deliver my newspapers." I kissed her and left.

On Sunday evening, I was watching TV in the den when the phone rang. I wasn't afraid that it might be Daddy, since he always called on Thursday nights. Besides, I *had* to answer the phone because Mom wasn't home and Corinne was in her room blasting her music.

"Hello," said an unfamiliar male voice. "Am I speaking to Corinne?" He sounded British and far away.

"No," I said. "This is Cassie."

"Oh, hello, Cassie." The man gave a good-natured chuckle. "You sound so mature, but I suppose you're no longer five, as you were the last time I saw you. This is your great-uncle Harry. How are you?"

"Hi, Uncle Harry," I said. "I'm fine. But how are you? Mom said you've been sick."

"Coming along." He lowered his voice. "If those silly nurses would only give me a moment's peace."

"Did you want to speak to Mom? She isn't here right now. She could call you back tomorrow if you like."

"I would like that very much," he said. "She has my telephone number. Tell her to reverse the charges. And tell her I've come up with a splendid idea that I want to discuss with her."

"Mom's out a lot. Any particular time you want her to call back?"

Uncle Harry gave a hoarse laugh that turned into a cough.

"Whenever she likes. I'm here day and night. Day and night," he repeated.

Mom spoke to Uncle Harry a few times that week. Each time he called, she talked to him on her bedroom extension. After one of his calls, Mom came into the kitchen, where I was doing my homework. She had a thoughtful expression on her face.

"Why are you talking to Uncle Harry so much lately?" I asked.

Mom gave me a funny look. "Oh, because we have a lot of catching up to do."

"But he's Daddy's uncle," I reminded her. "Not yours."

"I know," Mom said. "Still, I'm very fond of him. And he is recovering from a heart attack, with no family to look after him. His only brother, your grandfather, is dead. So is Uncle Harry's wife. They were very devoted to each other and never had any children."

"I hardly remember him from the last time he visited. He lives in Philadelphia, doesn't he?"

"Right you are," Mom said.

"Is he coming to visit us?"

Mom bit her lip and looked as if she couldn't decide how to answer me. "Maybe. We'll see."

Daddy's check came in the mail on Friday. Mom and I danced around the kitchen. "Things are beginning to fall into place," she said.

The following Wednesday, Daddy called to tell Corinne not to come to Louisville. Corasue had broken her leg and wasn't up to having company. They talked about her visiting during spring vacation. I could see that Corinne had tears in her eyes as she handed Mom the receiver.

"Here, Mom. Daddy wants to speak to you."

Mom looked guiltily at Corinne and me. "I'll take it in my bedroom."

Corinne and I exchanged glances. "What's going on?" I asked.

"Beats me," Corinne said angrily. "But I hope Mom gets off the telephone soon. If I'm not going to Daddy's, I might as well make the best of staying home. I want to call Jason and tell him I'll be able to go to the New Year's Eve parties with him, after all."

Mom, however, stayed on the phone for the next half hour. Corinne kept picking up the kitchen extension. She started pouting.

"I can't believe she's been talking to Daddy all this time," I said.

Corinne shook her head. "It's not Daddy. Sounds like some old man."

"Uncle Harry," I said. "Why is she always talking to Uncle Harry?"

Friday evening, we found out. Corinne and I were jabbering away over dinner. Ten whole days of Christmas vacation lay before us, and we were planning what we wanted to do.

"I want to go into Manhattan to see the Christmas tree at Rockefeller Center."

"And shop and look at all the store windows!" Corinne added. "Can we, Mom? Can we go into the city one day?"

"We'll see," Mom said.

Mom was quiet all through dinner. Her mind seemed to

be on other things. After she stacked the dishes in the dishwasher, she called Corinne and me into the den. We sat on the couch and watched as Mom paced before us, both of us wondering what she was about to say.

"Girls, I've been thinking of having Uncle Harry stay with us for a month or so. Until he gets back on his feet."

Corinne and I were so shocked, for a moment we couldn't speak.

"But, Mom," Corinne wailed, "that's a terrible idea. He's sick and needs someone to take care of him. Cassie and I are in school, and you're not here half the time."

Mom gave her a meaningful look. "I know I'm not. Even though you're not babies, I don't like the idea of leaving the two of you on your own so much."

I hated the idea even more than Corinne did. Ick! Having some stranger, some *man* wandering about our house, intruding on our privacy.

"You should have asked our opinion," I told Mom. "I mean, Corinne and I don't want him here."

"I didn't ask for your opinions, Cassie, because it's not for you to decide," Mom said. She sounded very stern. "I've come to my own conclusion after some good, hard thinking. Your father agrees with me on this."

"What do you care what Daddy thinks?" I asked, but Mom ignored me.

"You needn't worry that you'll have to take care of Uncle Harry," she said. "His nurses left yesterday, and he's able to get around the house and make his own breakfast and lunch. Remember, he's lived on his own for years."

"But where's he going to stay?" Corinne asked. "In the den? Does that mean Jason and I can't watch TV there?"

"No, you'll be able to watch TV in the den." Mom took a

deep breath and looked at Corinne, then at me. I knew something even worse was coming.

"I've decided it would be best to put Uncle Harry in Cassie's room. Cassie, you'll sleep on the extra bed in Corinne's room."

"What?" Corinne and I screamed at once.

"You can't do that, Mom," Corinne moaned. "I hardly have enough room as it is."

"We'll only fight and get on each other's nerves worse than ever," I said. My heart was sinking. Give up my room! I'd always had my own room, and the only one I had to share it with was Tom.

"How can you do this, Mom?" Corinne sniffed. She was crying. "You should have asked us. It's worse for us than for you."

Mom put her hand on Corinne's shoulder, but my sister shrugged it away. "Honey, I know how hard this is on you and Cassie. But, aside from everything I've said so far, we need the money. Uncle Harry's well-off. He came up with the idea of staying here, and he's insisting on paying me handsomely. He wants to live in a home, with family, while he's regaining his strength. And, girls, that's us."

"I think it's rotten of you to give him my room," I shouted.

"I would have put him in the den, but it's too open," Mom answered calmly. "There's nowhere else he can stay. Try and be understanding, Cassie. When you were younger, you were very fond of him."

"When is he coming?" Corinne asked.

"Sunday afternoon. You'll have all day tomorrow to reorganize your rooms."

CHAPTER 9

I couldn't believe Mom was actually driving me from my room. It was the only place where I could be alone to think or read or do whatever I felt like doing. And to give up my room to a *man*! Sure, we needed the money, but why did *I* have to be the one to make the sacrifice because Uncle Harry was coming?

The first thing Corinne said when Mom left us was that she wasn't having any mangy cat sleeping in her room.

"Mom," I wailed, chasing after her. "Corinne says Tom can't sleep with me in her room. Tell her —"

Mom turned around and snapped, "You two work things out for yourselves. I can't be settling your problems every minute of the day."

"But, Mom," I complained, shocked by her outburst. "That's not fair. You can't —" I stopped short outside Mom's bedroom as she shut the door in my face.

"Why don't you let Uncle Harry have *your* room, since you're so concerned?" I shouted at her through the closed door. "You could sleep in the den, and Corinne and I wouldn't have to argue."

Mom didn't answer, and I went into my room to sulk. My room. Ha! It was as if I were staying in a hotel, with the next guest arriving tomorrow.

I needed to talk to Bobby. He'd understand exactly what I was going through, I told myself as I hurried over to his house in the darkness. He hated it when his mother touched anything in his bedroom, or when Kenny wandered in.

"Cassie!" Mrs. Schaeffer looked surprised when she let me in.

I could see why. Suitcases were open in the living room and the den.

"Hi, Mrs. Schaeffer. You're going to Aruba tomorrow," I said, suddenly remembering.

"That's right! The taxi's coming for us at six-thirty in the morning. Go on upstairs. Bobby's packing. Oh, one more thing," she said, smiling. "Don't forget to stop our paper for a week. But be sure to check the mailbox tomorrow."

Bobby's room was a disaster area, with clothes all over his bed, the bureau, the chair. He was at his desk figuring out a math problem. He grinned when he saw me.

"Hi, Cassie. What's up?"

I moved some clothes over and sat down on the bed. "Nothing good. Daddy's uncle Harry is coming to stay with us. He's taking over my room."

"How come?"

"He's recovering from a heart attack. Isn't that the worst?"

"Well, I'd sure hate to lose my room. But I bet Uncle Harry's only staying for a while. As soon as he's well, you'll have your room back. Be patient."

"Be patient?" I shrieked. "You try and be patient. I should have known better than to come here. You're defending Uncle Harry because he's a man."

Bobby shook his head. "You're not going to start that business again, are you?"

"I wish I could live someplace where there were no men. Where no boys were allowed."

"Cassie!"

"Have a great time in Aruba, Bobby," I said. "Don't think of me suffering here." Without a backward glance, I stomped out of his room and headed for home.

I delivered my papers in record time Saturday morning, since lots of people were away on vacation. The nice thing was, almost everyone handed me a Christmas tip or left one for me in the mailbox, as Mrs. Schaeffer had. Lucky Bobby, I thought as I rode to the next house. Swimming and snorkeling in the sun while I had to bunk with Corinne. Ick!

When I got home, Corinne's CD player was blasting as usual. She shouted above the noise to tell me she'd made room for me in her closet and her bureau. I could start moving my stuff in anytime I wanted, because she was going to the mall with Jason. Mom, I was glad to see, was out at a last-minute dress rehearsal for that evening's performance.

I waited until Corinne left the house before I started putting my things into her room. In her typically selfish way, she hadn't given me much space. I couldn't possibly bring in everything I'd need — only my schoolbooks and my underwear and the clothes I wore most of the time. I cleared out four drawers and half of my closet for Uncle Harry. He'd have to make do with that.

I took down my WOMEN ONLY sign, since Mom would have a fit if she saw it still hanging on my door. Then I got my stamp album and slipped it under the bed I'd be using in Corinne's room.

I stormed from room to room, slamming doors and grumbling. Nothing was working out. Nothing! The vacation was here, and I had plenty of time to work on my album. The trouble was, I'd already gone through the packet and put all of the stamps that I could into the album. If only I could get to the stamp store in Glen Haven and buy more stamps.

I could get there by bus, I suddenly realized. I'd have plenty of time next week. Why shouldn't I do what *I* wanted for a change?

Uncle Harry arrived at five o'clock the next day. He came by limousine, which must have cost a small fortune. He was thin and stooped, with a bony face and a large bald head that made him look like an ancient baby. He squinted a lot, even though he wore glasses. But when he smiled, his blue eyes sparkled with glee.

Uncle Harry seemed really glad to be here. First he kissed Mom, then shook hands with Corinne and me while the limousine driver brought in his luggage.

"It's wonderful seeing all of you again. I can't tell you how happy I am to be here," Uncle Harry said, beaming all around — at us, the house, even Tom. He handed each of us a gift-wrapped package. "A little something for the holidays."

"Oh, Uncle Harry," said Mom. "You shouldn't have." But she ripped hers open as fast as a little kid would, and oohed and aahed as she unfolded the cream-colored silk blouse inside. Corinne joined in the sound effects when she saw her brown leather gloves. She tried them on and said they fitted perfectly.

My gift was the biggest package of all. I stared down at it. Three sets of eyes were on me. I wished I could run into my room and slam the door, shutting everyone out. I didn't want a present from Uncle Harry, but I couldn't hurt his feelings. Not with him watching me and grinning.

I opened my present and couldn't hide my outrage when I saw what was inside. A black-and-white stuffed animal. A dog. Something for a two-year-old.

Uncle Harry noticed my expression and started to apologize. "I'm sorry, Cassie. I suppose you're too old for stuffed animals, but the salesclerk assured me that girls of all ages love them."

"I love stuffed animals," Corinne told him, "even if Cassie doesn't."

"Well, then, *you* can keep it," I said. "Here!" I shoved the dog into her hands and flew downstairs to the basement.

Mom let me cool off for a while before she came down to talk to me. Mostly, it was a lecture about how I shouldn't have been rude to Uncle Harry, because he meant well.

"He hasn't seen you since you were five. How is he supposed to know you don't like stuffed animals?"

"I'm not a baby, Mom," I said.

"I know, honey. Let's all just try to get through this, okay?"

"Sure," I agreed, the fight gone from me. "I'll apologize to Uncle Harry," I said before she could tell me to do so.

"Thanks, Cassie," Mom said, and kissed my cheek. She went upstairs, leaving me feeling more alone and misunderstood than ever. Daddy would have known what I was going through, I thought as tears trickled down my cheeks. Daddy would have found a way to make me feel better.

A half hour later, I knocked on my own bedroom door. I spit out my apology as quickly as possible. Uncle Harry took it very nicely.

"I should have realized you were a serious young lady." He looked down at Tom, who was staring at him and probably wondering what Uncle Harry was doing in our room. "One who prefers cats to dogs."

I couldn't help smiling as I took Tom into my arms.

"And, Cassie," he called when I was halfway out of the door. "Thanks for letting me use your room. I know what a sacrifice that must be for you. For anyone." He gave a little laugh. "To tell the truth, I don't know if *I* could bring myself to do it."

"That's because you don't have a mother to make you," I said over my shoulder. For a moment, I wondered if I'd insulted him. But he was laughing as I closed the door behind me.

It was funny how Uncle Harry didn't take up as much space in the house as I thought he would. Most of the time, he ate breakfast and lunch earlier than we did. He stayed in my room reading or in the den watching TV. He joined us for dinner, and while he listened to everything that was said and made comments as well, he never tried to take over the conversation. I found I was angrier at Mom than at Uncle Harry, because she was the one who didn't care about my feelings. Mom pretended not to know I was angry at her, and acted as though everything were fine between us.

Monday was Christmas day. During dinner that evening, Mom and Corinne made plans to go into Manhattan. "Let's go in on Wednesday," Mom said, beaming at both of us. "We'll do some shopping, eat lunch, maybe take in a movie. How does that sound, girls?"

"Great, Mom," Corinne said. "Will we take the train or drive?"

"The train, I think," Mom answered. "I couldn't face all that holiday traffic."

"I can't wait!" Corinne said.

"Okay with you, Cassie?"

"I guess."

Mom sighed. "Try and enjoy the vacation, Cassie, instead of making yourself miserable."

Me make myself miserable! That was a good one. But I didn't want to start an argument and get another lecture, so I just sat there glowering.

I waited until Wednesday morning to tell Mom I wouldn't be going into the city with her and Corinne. I came into the kitchen as they were finishing breakfast.

"Hurry up, slowpoke," Corinne said. "We want to make the ten o'clock train."

"I'm not going with you," I told them.

"Why not?" Mom asked. "Don't you feel well?"

"Not that great," I fibbed. "But you two go ahead."

Mom looked at me doubtfully. "What's wrong, Cassie? Does your throat hurt? Do you think you have a fever?"

I squirmed, hating to lie. "I guess I'm a little tired. And I still have to deliver my papers."

Mom bit her lip. "I wonder if *we* should go in. They predict snow this evening."

"Only flurries, Mom," Corinne said. "And they always say that. Half the time, they're wrong."

"I know, but just the possibility of snow makes me nervous," Mom said.

"Come on, Mom, stop worrying," Corinne pleaded. "It never snows much in Manhattan. Besides, today's the only vacation day we're both free."

Mom thought a minute, then turned up her hands. "Oh, you're probably right." She looked at me. "And you'll have

Uncle Harry to keep you company. You can heat up the leftovers from yesterday if we're not home by six o'clock."

"Sure, Mom," I said, glad to have gotten out of the trip so easily. "Have a good time."

I decided to take the eleven-thirty bus to Glen Haven. I was excited as I put on my jeans and sweater, brushed my hair, and told Uncle Harry I was going out for a few hours.

The sky was gray-white, and the wind chilled my ears as I waited on the corner of Main and Fifth Street for the bus to come.

"It sure looks like snow," the fat woman standing next to me mumbled.

"I guess," I answered. "But it won't snow until tonight. At least, that's what they said on the radio."

The woman shook her head. "I don't know. My shoulder's hurting pretty bad. And my shoulder's never wrong."

Just then, the bus came into sight and we climbed aboard. I paid my fare and took my ticket. According to the schedule, the trip from Townsend to Glen Haven took twenty-eight minutes, but I asked the driver just to be sure.

"We'll pull in two minutes before noon. Check your watch and see if I'm wrong," he said proudly. "I always make it before the noon siren goes off."

His words reassured me and helped me forget about the fat woman's aching shoulder. I didn't have anything to worry about. I'd get to Glen Haven at twelve, stay an hour at the most, and be home before three o'clock, well before Mom and Corinne returned from Manhattan.

CHAPTER 10

T he stamp store, which also sold coins, was kept locked, so I had to ring a buzzer to be let in. Two men sat on stools inside a square formed by glass-covered counters. The older man, who was olive-skinned and bald and had a mustache, was busy reorganizing the coins under one of the counters. The younger man wore a suit and had a sneering expression. His beady eyes reminded me of a bird on the lookout for worms. "Can I help you?" he asked, sounding as unpleasant as he looked.

"Yes, well, I want to buy some stamps for my album," I explained, nervous because of his manner. "International stamps. From all over."

"I see." He sniffed disapprovingly. "Can you be a little more specific?"

He was making it difficult for me. Soon I'd start babbling like a two-year-old. That happened sometimes when I had to speak to unpleasant strangers or in front of a lot of people.

The buzzer rang, and an elderly couple came into the store. The bald, mustached man locked the showcase he'd been working on and turned to the nasty young man.

"Don, the Mastersons are back. Why don't you take care of them while I look after this young lady?" He nodded to me. "I'll be with you in one moment."

A minute later, he came around the counter and offered me his hand. "Now, what can I do for you? I'm Emilio Flores, the owner of this establishment." His voice was soft and musical, with a slight Spanish accent.

"I'm Cassie Landauer. I want to get more stamps for my album," I explained, regaining my confidence as I spoke. "It's kind of old. Actually, it was my father's. I've already bought one packet and I'm not sure what to do next."

"I see." Mr. Flores rested his chin in his hand as he thought. "You didn't bring your album with you?"

"No, I didn't. Should I have?"

"Well, maybe next time. Who told you to come to us? Or did you just happen to drop in?"

"Mr. Guerney from the Townsend Post Office said I should stop by. That was months ago, but I haven't been able to get here till now."

"Alfie Guerney sent you." Mr. Flores grinned. "Then I'd better take good care of you, or he'll come here on his lunch hour and give me a piece of his mind."

By now I knew that Mr. Flores would take good care of me, regardless of how I happened to come to his store. "Is it okay if I just look around first?" I asked. "I've never been in a stamp store before."

"Certainly. Let me start off by showing you our most expensive stamp. It's worth twenty thousand dollars in today's market."

Mr. Flores unlocked a case and took out a beautifully colored stamp of a bird with a long tail. The stamp was from Central America. He went into a long explanation of why it was so expensive. Then he showed me all kinds of stamps. There were pictures of animals, of famous people, of sports, of mountains. Mr. Flores told me that a stamp accidentally printed upside down or with a part missing was worth a lot of money.

"They're exquisite," I sighed, after he put away a sheet of commemorative stamps from France. "I wish I had enough money to buy them."

Mr. Flores laughed good-naturedly. "When you're older, perhaps. But what would you like to get today?"

"I don't know. I still have so many blank spaces in my album."

"Then perhaps you would like to buy another packet."

"Do you think so?" I told him how many stamps there were in the first packet.

"This time you might want to buy a larger packet," he said. "But I must warn you to be prepared for doubles."

"That's okay. I also need to add pages to my album for countries that weren't around thirty years ago."

"Certainly."

I remembered a few other items I wanted, and Mr. Flores got them for me. Then he figured out my bill. I had enough money to pay for everything, with five dollars to spare.

"You're developing a fine appreciation of stamps," Mr. Flores said as he handed me my package. "I bet you'd enjoy going to the big stamp show in Manhattan. Dealers come from all over the world. What wonderful stamps you would see!" He put his hand over his heart. "I intend to be there."

"When is the show?" I asked.

"The end of March. Try to go." He smiled. "If you do, you're in for a real treat."

We shook hands, and I promised to stop by the post office and give Mr. Guerney his regards. I left the store with the feeling I'd made a real friend.

Outside, flurries were falling from a sunless sky. Thank goodness they melted as soon as they reached the ground. My watch said one-thirty, which meant I'd spent an hour and a half in the stamp store. And what a worthwhile time it had been! I'd learned more about stamps from Mr. Flores than from all the books I'd read over the past few months. I hugged my package close. I couldn't wait to get home and sort through the stamps in my new packet. My next step, as Mr. Flores had suggested, would be to order stamps from catalogs. I liked the idea of using catalogs, because then I could choose exactly what I wanted.

My stomach began to growl, and I realized that I hadn't eaten lunch. I took out my bus schedule. A bus left for Townsend at two-ten. Great. I had plenty of time to get a sandwich and something warm to drink.

I found a coffee shop halfway down the block from Mr. Flores's store. I sat at the counter and ate my tuna sandwich and drank my hot chocolate. I checked the addition of my bill the way Daddy always did, then figured out a fifteen percent tip. I was proud of myself for getting to Glen Haven and buying what I needed. I felt grown-up and ready for life: for high school, driving a car, working. And best of all, for being on my own.

I headed back to the bus stop with five minutes to spare. It was snowing harder now. My sneakers left footprints on the white sidewalk. No one was waiting at the bus stop, but I didn't think much about it — not until ten minutes had passed. Then I thought I'd better go into the bus depot and see what was wrong. Maybe the bus was delayed because of the weather.

Inside, a toothless man on duty laughed loudly when I asked him when the two-ten bus was expected to arrive.

"It's come and gone, missy."

"But how can that be?" I asked, upset. "I was there at two-ten. At five after two, in fact."

"You must have just missed it. That Joe." He shook his head from side to side so hard, I thought it would come off. "I keep telling him not to leave early, but he says everyone knows to be at the bus ten minutes earlier."

"Well, I didn't know that," I said. "I was going by my bus schedule. He shouldn't have left so early."

The man shrugged. "I keep telling Joe the very same thing, but it does no good." He smiled. "Cheer up. Another bus should be along in an hour or so."

"An hour!" I exclaimed. "That will be a quarter after three. And it's beginning to snow hard."

"Sorry, missy," the man said sympathetically. "Maybe you want to call your parents to pick you up."

I shook my head. I still had a good chance of getting home before Mom and Corinne. If I called now, Uncle Harry would tell Mom and I'd get into trouble for going so far without permission. Besides, I didn't want to worry Uncle Harry. He probably thought I was at a friend's house.

It was close to four o'clock when the bus finally arrived. The driver was the same one who had brought me to Glen Haven. Snow was falling steadily, blanketing the streets and everything in sight as we lumbered along. I couldn't count the times I feared that we'd get stuck in a snowdrift or that a skidding car would crash into us.

When I wasn't worrying about some physical disaster, I brooded about Mom worrying about me. I should have called home. Mom was probably back from Manhattan, frantic and wondering where I was. Snow made Mom crazy. She'd been in a car accident during a blizzard when she was little. Now, as soon as the flakes started sticking and one of us wasn't home, she always imagined the worst. She might even think I was dead.

I arrived in Townsend two hours later. The short walk to our house seemed like a five-mile trek. The wind blew snow in my face so that I could hardly see. My feet were wet and numb with cold. I hoped I didn't have frostbite.

At last, I stood outside my house. I tucked my stamp package under my chin and was searching in my pockets for my key when the door flew open and Mom grabbed me.

"Cassie! Where on earth have you been? I've called everyone I could think of. The police. The hospitals. Thank God, you're all right." Mom looked me over. "You *are* all right, aren't you?"

My teeth were chattering as I shook myself out of my jacket and kicked off my wet sneakers. Corinne and Uncle Harry came to stare at me.

"I'm fine, Mom," I said. "And I'm sorry for upsetting you."

"But where have you been?" Mom screeched. "You said you didn't feel well and didn't want to go to the city with us." I followed her into the kitchen, where she put the kettle on to boil. "I'll make you some hot chocolate and hope you don't get pneumonia."

"I — I took the bus to Glen Haven, and it was delayed coming home." I hesitated, on the verge of telling Mom why I'd gone there, when she went berserk. Her face paled and her eyes were so wide and bulging, I thought they'd pop out.

"Now, isn't that the limit! You couldn't go into the city with Corinne and me, but you were well enough to traipse off by yourself! And on a day like today. You knew how nervous I was about the weather."

"But, Mom, it wasn't supposed to snow until tonight. That was why you went —"

"Don't tell me what I did," Mom snapped. "You didn't even have the decency to call us."

Just then, the phone rang. Mom spoke in polite tones. "Yes, she's here, officer. Thank you." Mom hung up and turned back to me.

"There! Even the Townsend Police were out looking for you." Mom shook her head sadly. "I don't know what to do with you, Cassie. First you take your father's remarriage as a personal insult, and now you're running wild."

"I'm not running wild, Mom. I just went to Glen Haven. You act like I took a plane to California or something."

"Don't act fresh, miss, or you'll be going to bed at eight o'clock until you're in high school."

I started to cry from exasperation. "You won't listen to anything I say, will you? I didn't mean to get back this late. I missed a bus because the driver left early, and the next bus was delayed. I should have called you, I know, but I thought —" I stopped when I saw that Mom's angry face hadn't softened.

"Oh, what's the use." I got my stamp package from the hall, then ran into Corinne's room and slammed the door shut. I was relieved to be alone.

A few minutes later, Corinne came in carrying a tray with a mug of hot chocolate and a sandwich. "I made you a tuna fish sandwich on a dinner roll," she said kindly, as if I were sick. "Sorry if it's skimpy, but there wasn't much tuna left."

"Thanks, Corinne," I said gratefully.

Corinne watched me gulp down the little sandwich in two bites before she added, "Mom's talking about taking you to see a psychiatrist. A woman Jessie heard of."

I stared at her. "You're kidding. All I did was take a bus to Glen Haven and return late. She never actually said I couldn't ever go to Glen Haven."

Corinne shrugged. "She says she's worried about you. About how you've changed since Daddy left."

"We've all changed," I said angrily. "She's only upset because of the snow."

"Well, you should have called. You've no idea how frantic she was."

"I *know* I should have called," I snapped.

"Don't yell at me, Cassie," Corinne said. "Maybe Mom's right. Maybe you do need to see a psychiatrist and find out why you're always angry."

Corinne left. I got into my pajamas and turned out the light. But even though I was thoroughly exhausted, I couldn't settle down. A terrible sadness came over me. I felt that, no matter what I said, I'd never be heard. Tears fell onto my hands, my quilt, my pajamas. I was so alone. Mom didn't understand me. Neither did Corinne or Bobby. The one person who did was far, far away.

I wanted my father. I wanted him to hug me and hold me and tell me it was adventurous but inconsiderate of me to have gone to Glen Haven. That I should have waited until he could have taken me there, just the two of us.

But now he'd never take me to Glen Haven to buy stamps.

Suddenly, I knew, just as Bobby had said all those months ago, that working on the stamp album was my way of remaining connected to my father. My own way, so secretive that I hadn't even realized it until now.

I started to sob, deep, wrenching sobs, as I mourned the loss of my father. Even if I did see him on holidays, even if I spoke to him every week as Corinne did, he would always be missing from the everyday part of my life. I covered my face with my pillow so no one could hear me crying.

I must have fallen asleep that way, because the next thing I knew, it was morning.

CHAPTER 11

I awoke early the next morning feeling happy. I could remember parts of a dream — being in a bicycle race and coming out the winner. I ran down to the basement to get Tom and fed him breakfast. He purred as he ate his dried food, and I felt like purring, too. Outside, the sun was shining on a snow-covered world — all clean and white and new. Yesterday's snowstorm and Mom's being upset had receded to the back of my mind. For the first time in as long as I could remember, I was looking forward to a wonderful day.

When I got to the kitchen, Mom and Uncle Harry were finishing their breakfast. "Good morning," I greeted them cheerfully. "It looks great out. I think I'll go sledding after I deliver my papers."

"Good morning, honey." Mom kissed my cheek. I could see that she was back to her old self, but I wasn't taking any chances.

"I'm sorry about yesterday, Mom," I said. "I shouldn't have gone to Glen Haven without telling you. I won't do it again."

Mom smiled. "I suppose I did overreact a bit. But you had all of us frightened. Didn't she, Harry?"

Uncle Harry nodded. "Only somehow I knew she was safe. I refrained from repeatedly saying so, Claudia, for fear of upsetting you more."

The three of us laughed at that. I called Melissa to find out if she wanted to go sledding. She thought it was a terrific idea. We talked a bit about Janie missing the snowfall because she was visiting her grandparents in Florida. Then Melissa arranged for her mom to drive us to Taylor's Hill.

Jason pulled into our driveway just as Melissa's mom was honking for me. He gave me a big wave as I came outside.

"Is that Corinne's boyfriend?" Melissa asked when she finished gawking at him.

"I guess so. Corinne's gaga over him," I said.

"I don't blame her. He's gorgeous." Melissa giggled.

"Jason's a soccer star. He plays varsity basketball, too," I informed her as casually as I could.

"Wow!" Melissa said. "I wish I had a beautiful older sister."

I was in a good mood, so I didn't bother rattling off Corinne's long list of character defects.

Melissa's mom dropped us off at Taylor's Hill. It seemed that everyone in Townsend had decided to go sledding that day. Kids called out to us, and we shouted back as we climbed the hill side by side. We laughed all the way down and chatted as we climbed up again. Melissa talked a lot about the sixth-grade yearbook, which was only natural since she was chairperson of the yearbook committee. Then she asked me if I wanted to room with her and Janie and another girl when we went to Washington.

"Sure I do," I told her. "But the trip's not until May."

"I know, but it's better to have everything arranged early," Melissa said.

I laughed. "You're the most planned-out person I know," I told her.

Mom came to pick us up. She was nice about waiting while we took one more run. In the car, Melissa asked, "Cassie, do you want to sleep over Saturday night?"

"Yes." I looked at Mom. "If it's okay with you."

Mom nodded. "It's fine with me, Cassie."

"Great," Melissa said. "We'll rent some DVDs to watch."

"And we'll get some popcorn," I reminded her. "Don't forget the popcorn."

"Would I forget the popcorn?" Melissa teased. "Me? The most planned-out person you know?"

I could tell that Mom was pleased I was doing things with Melissa. She hummed all the way home.

I changed out of my wet clothes, then went into the kitchen to make hot chocolate. Corinne and Jason were there, having an argument. Jason was trying to explain something while my sister paced up and down like a caged tiger.

"Hi, Cassie," Jason greeted me. "Have a good time sledding?"

"It was terrific. I just want to make some hot chocolate," I explained. "I'll be gone in a minute."

Corinne ignored me. "Jason, all I'm asking is that you come to the mall with me for half an hour tomorrow. No longer, I promise."

"And all I'm saying is, I've had it with going to the mall," Jason answered. "I hate shopping, Corinne. Can't you understand that?" He was being polite, but even I could tell he was annoyed. "Hey, let's give Cassie a break and go into the den."

Corinne gave me one of her killing looks, but she followed him out.

I stayed over at Melissa's house Saturday night and took a long nap on Sunday to make up for all the sleep I missed. The next day, I went with Mom to Nancy and Jeff's annual New Year's Day party.

"I don't understand," I said on the way over to Nancy's house, "why two divorced people give parties together."

Mom laughed. "People do all kinds of crazy things. Some even remarry once or twice." She gave me a worried look. "Not that it would ever happen with your father and me, so don't expect it to, even in your wildest dreams."

"Oh, I know," I said, as though she'd said something really silly. But I had thought that exact thing once or twice — imagining Corasue died or Daddy divorced her — all the while knowing it couldn't come true.

Jeff greeted us at the door, and I was a little embarrassed to see him. He gave me a big smile and wished me a Happy New Year as if I'd never put up a sign ordering him to leave our house. Still, I was glad that although he kissed Mom hello, he didn't act like he was in love with her or anything.

Jeff introduced me to his daughter, who was in the sixth grade like me. We talked a bit, but after a while I got something to eat and wandered back to Mom. She sat with a group of people in the living room, looking pretty in the new blouse Uncle Harry had given her. She put her arm around me, and everyone shifted to make room for me on the couch.

"I'd like you all to meet my daughter Cassie. Cassie, this is Tom, Allie, Phyllis, Robbie, and Sam." I smiled as Mom introduced each person, even though I knew I wouldn't remember anyone's name. Except for Sam's. He looked younger than the others, tall and thin, with intense brown eyes and a shy smile. I was content to sit beside Mom, half listening to the conversation and sipping my soda. Everyone liked Mom, I could tell. Especially Sam.

We left around six o'clock. Mom kissed everyone goodbye, and I thanked Jeff and Nancy for having us. In the car, I told Mom, "I think Sam likes you."

"Do you, honey?" Mom answered. And she began to hum.

The vacation was over. After being in school for one hour Tuesday morning, I felt as if it had never happened. At lunch, Janie told Melissa and me all about her vacation in Florida. I thought of Bobby and wondered how he'd liked Aruba. Wondered, too, if he was still mad at me for yelling at him. I only yelled at him because he kept on saying the wrong things. If he was mad, that was tough. Let him stay mad! I certainly wasn't about to apologize to any *boy*.

But when I came home after delivering my papers, and Uncle Harry said that Bobby was waiting for me in the den, I went in and threw my arms around him. I was so glad to see him.

"How was Aruba?" I asked.

Bobby grinned. "Great! I went snorkeling, and I brought back some cool shells and rock samples." He looked pretty good himself, with his nice, even tan. For a moment, I felt a stab of jealousy because he could go on vacations when I couldn't anymore. Then I noticed he was holding something out to me.

"Here, Cassie, I got you something."

I unwrapped a mug with a colorful bird and *Aruba* painted on it. "Gee, thanks." I was touched.

"It's kind of a make-up gift," Bobby said, sitting down on the couch. "I wish we wouldn't fight anymore."

"Me, too." I put the mug on the table and sat beside him.

"How was your vacation?" Bobby asked.

"Okay." I told him about the trip to Glen Haven and going sledding with Melissa.

Bobby looked around to see if we were alone. "Your uncle Harry seems like a nice guy. How are things working out?"

I shrugged. "Not too bad, I guess."

Bobby grinned. "See, I told you it wouldn't be as awful as you thought."

His cocky attitude annoyed me. "It's still far from great, Bobby. You don't know what it's like to have a stranger move into your house. To have to share a room with Corinne."

"I had to share a room with Kenny for a week."

"Big fat deal," I told him. "You were on vacation. I probably won't get to leave Townsend until I go away to college."

"You could always visit your father in Kentucky."

I stared at him, not believing he was harping on *that* again. Bobby gave me a searching look.

"Have you thought about it, Cass? Going to see your father?"

"There's nothing to think about," I said, fighting hard to control the fury building up inside me. "I won't see him, and that's that."

"You made your point, Cassie," Bobby went on. "He knows you're angry — he knows you're hurt."

I shook my head.

"Do it for your own sake," he persisted. "You need your father, whether you admit it or not."

"No, I don't, Bobby Schaeffer! I don't need Daddy. I don't need any man in my life, and that includes you!"

"Cassie, cut it out."

"Go on, leave. No boys allowed in this house!"

Bobby stood up. "You really mean it, don't you? All this time I thought you were half-kidding, but you're not." He strode toward the front door. "I've had it! You can find yourself another best friend, Cassie. Someone who isn't a boy!"

Shocked, I watched Bobby leave. I almost yelled after him to say I was sorry and I didn't mean what I'd said. But I *did* mean it. Every word of it. Bobby sided with Daddy and Uncle Harry because they were males. They all stuck together. Well, I had Melissa and Janie and all the other sixth-grade girls to be friendly with! I didn't need Bobby Schaeffer around.

Thursday afternoon was the first chance I had to look through my new stamps. I closed the door to Corinne's room and pulled the packet from under my bed. I had plenty of time because Corinne was at one of Jason's basketball games and Mom wouldn't be home until late. Uncle Harry was probably in the den watching TV.

I opened the packet and sprinkled some stamps onto the carpet just to get a look at them. Then I simply had to go through my album to see if I had any of those stamps. Out of ten, only one was a double. Excited, I poured a whole bunch of stamps onto the floor. France fell on top of Argentina, Canada on Afghanistan. What fun I was going to have mounting all these stamps! And I had to remember to put in the new pages I'd bought. Maybe I should do that first.

There was a knock on the door. I stared at the stamps and Daddy's album in dismay. Before I could hide everything, the door opened. Uncle Harry came in.

"Sorry to disturb you, Cassie, but I didn't know if you heard me. I wanted to know where your mother keeps the —"

He stopped when he caught the look of outrage on my face.

"Did I interrupt something?" Uncle Harry asked. "I apologize. I shouldn't have barged in like that."

"It's all right," I mumbled, gathering up the loose stamps on the carpet.

"But you collect stamps!" he exclaimed. "I must say, you've kept that a secret, haven't you?"

He was so on target, I blushed.

"Yeah, well," I said, thinking fast. "I haven't had much of a chance to work on my album lately."

I tried to push Daddy's album under the bed, but Uncle Harry reached down to look at it.

"Do you mind?"

I shrugged, wishing I could say that I did.

"This is rather an old album. Hmm." He leafed through the pages. I felt like grabbing it away. Instead, I clenched my hands into fists.

"If this doesn't look exactly like the album I gave your father. Though it's so many years . . ." I held my breath as Uncle Harry turned to the inside cover. "It *is* the same album! Here's the date." A dazzling smile lit up his face. "Why, I watched your father write it in." He laughed. "I even loaned him my pen to do it."

"You actually remember that after thirty years?" I asked.

"Of course I do," he said proudly. "As clear as if it were yesterday."

Uncle Harry sat on the bed. His eyes seemed to look inward, to faraway memories of when my father was a boy and Uncle Harry was no older than my father was now. What was it like, I wondered, to be living in London in the seventies? I glanced up at my great-uncle from where I still sat cross-legged on the floor.

"Tell me about it," I said softly.

Uncle Harry stroked his cheek and gave a little laugh. "Well, it was the week before Colin and his parents were leaving for America. Your grandfather, who was my older brother, and I decided it would be best if we moved the family business to the United States."

He shrugged. "It didn't mean much to me and your great-aunt Gertrude. Gertrude." He shook his head, grinning. "She wouldn't have minded if I said we were moving to Africa. But it was hard on your grandmother." Uncle Harry shot me a keen look. "And on your father, especially. He had his life in London — school, friends, a pet dog named Binky that he adored. But a child has nothing to say in these matters."

I knew *that* all too well. "Poor Daddy. Is that why you bought him this album? To help take his mind off leaving?"

Uncle Harry nodded. "And the people and places he was leaving behind. Colin loved the album. When we moved to the States, your father became an avid stamp collector — just like you." He got up. "Well, I'll leave you to your sorting, or whatever you were doing when I interrupted."

He was almost out of the room when I called, "Uncle Harry?"

He turned. "Hmm?"

"Please don't mention to anyone that I have the album — like Mom or Corinne, okay?"

"Sure thing, Cassie. By the way, I never did get to ask you where Claudia keeps things like tissues. I used up the box in your room."

79

I laughed. "She doesn't. Just write *tissues* on the list on the bulletin board and hope Mom gets them the next time she's out shopping. Take these, Uncle Harry." I pulled up a handful from the box on Corinne's night table.

I sat on the floor and pictured Daddy, eleven years old, leaving his home and his friends to go to America. How scared and lonely he must have been. To think he'd brought his stamp album with him, the very stamp album that was now mine. I picked up the album and pressed it to my heart. It felt good to know he'd loved collecting, same as I did.

CHAPTER 12

I t was the coldest January that anyone could remember. The temperature stayed in the teens. It snowed a lot, and we had two days off from school. "One more snow day," Mr. Olson sternly announced over the P.A. system, "and we will lose a day of spring vacation." That made all of us in Mrs. Morris's class laugh. Mr. Olson was treating the weather like a student who'd been acting up in class.

Every afternoon, I hurried home from school so I could deliver my newspapers as quickly as possible. I considered getting rid of my route because of the bad weather. And also because it felt strange delivering Bobby's paper now that we weren't talking. I worried that he would open the front door just as I dropped off the paper, but he never did.

In the end, I kept my job because of the money. Mom said that since Uncle Harry was staying with us as a paying guest, I could keep all that I earned. I was glad about that. Once I started buying stamps through catalogs, I'd need every cent I had.

That month, I found a different place to work on my stamp

collection. The day after Uncle Harry had found me working on Daddy's album, he called to me from the kitchen. I'd
just returned from my route and was stamping snow from
my boots.

"Why don't you come in here and have some hot chocolate?"

Why not? I thought. My fingers and toes were so frozen,
I could hardly feel them. I sat down at the table. A mug of
hot chocolate and some cookies were at my place. I downed
them as quickly as I could without burning my lips on the
hot chocolate. Soon I was feeling warm and cozy.

"Thanks a lot, Uncle Harry," I said, meaning it. I started
to get up.

"Did you have a good day at school?" he asked.

"Not bad. We had a social studies quiz, and then some of
us read our book reports out loud. I got to read mine." I
smiled, remembering. "Mrs. Morris said I understood the
true gist of the story."

"Ah, reading." Uncle Harry had a faraway look. "How I
loved to read when I was your age." He chuckled. "I en-
joyed it so much, I would turn on my lamp when I was supposed to be sleeping. I'd put a sheet over it so my parents
couldn't see the light." He shook his head. "Looking back,
it's a wonder I didn't start a fire."

I grinned. "I use a flashlight. It's safer."

We both laughed at that. I started getting up again. Uncle
Harry said, "Why don't you work on your album here in
the kitchen? You can spread out everything on the table."

"I don't know," I said doubtfully. I didn't want Mom or
Corrine walking in on me and asking me about my new
hobby.

Uncle Harry knew what was bothering me. "Go on,

Cassie," he said. "I'll be in the den. From there I can see anyone approaching the house." He winked. "I'll be your lookout, as they say."

I thought a bit. It *would* be easier working on the kitchen
table. And if Corinne or Mom came home earlier than expected, I could sweep everything onto the open album and
slip it under my bed in one minute flat.

"Offer accepted," I said.

"Then I'll take up my position."

And so, on afternoons when both Mom and Corinne were
out — which was most of the time — Uncle Harry and I fell
into a routine. I'd have my hot chocolate and cookies while
Uncle Harry drank his herbal tea and some dietetic cake he
was allowed to eat. Uncle Harry would ask me about my
day in school, which somehow always led to other things. A
few times we talked about Daddy.

"What was Daddy like when he was little?" I asked.

Uncle Harry scrunched up his forehead and thought. "Let
me try to remember." After a while, he said, "Colin was shy,
for one thing. And afraid of lightning."

"Daddy was afraid of lightning?" I said, astonished. My
father wasn't afraid of anything that I knew of.

"Indeed he was," Uncle Harry said. "Once when I was
visiting, lightning lit up the entire house. Your father let out
a scream and ran to hide under his bed with Binky right behind him."

We had a good chuckle over that. I liked hearing stories
about Daddy when he was young. He sounded sensitive. A
little bit like Bobby — before Bobby got so know-it-all and
bossy.

One nice thing about Uncle Harry was that he understood I needed time to work on my album. After we chatted

a while, he'd say, "You probably have things to do, so I'll go and watch the telly in the den." And he'd give me a wink, which meant he'd let me know if Mom or Corinne was coming home.

Most of the time, I was glad that Uncle Harry had turned out to be such a great person and that we could talk and have fun. Other times, I scolded myself for being friendly with the enemy. There was no getting away from it — Uncle Harry was a *man*. He was a member of the sex I'd sworn never to talk to again, never to depend on or to care about because men couldn't be trusted. But Uncle Harry's old, I'd remind myself, and he's recovering from a heart attack.

And he was a guest in my house, so I had to be polite to him, didn't I?

Corinne and Jason were an "item," as my sister put it. He had given her his basketball jacket New Year's Eve, and Corinne wore it all the time around the house. When she wasn't with Jason, she was on the telephone with him. And when she wasn't with him or talking to him, she was talking *about* him. It was nauseating.

Sometimes, when Jason didn't have basketball practice, he and Corinne would stay in the house and just hang out. It was different when they were around. Uncle Harry and I didn't talk about the things we usually talked about. And of course I didn't work on my stamp album. Although the lovebirds usually stayed in the den, they seemed to take over the entire house. Uncle Harry and I could hear them from the kitchen, laughing and kidding around. We'd make faces at each other when things got quiet and we figured they were probably kissing.

Although I knew Corinne and Jason really liked each

other, by the end of January, they were always arguing. They argued over a lot of things, but mainly because Corinne would want Jason to go someplace or do something that he didn't want to do. A few times Jason stormed out of our house, slamming the door behind him. Still, he always called that night, and Corinne would speak to him on the extension in Mom's room. I never found out what he said, but he must have given in to Corinne, because each time, she came out of Mom's bedroom with a smile of triumph on her face.

Uncle Harry would shake his head whenever Jason left our house after a quarrel. "This can't go on forever," he would mumble. "Someone should talk to that young lady."

"Let Corinne get what she wants," I said. "Men should have to do what women like, for a change." Still, I felt guilty even as I spoke. I knew Corrine was acting selfish and unreasonable, and wasn't being fair to Jason.

Uncle Harry and I became good friends. He was easygoing and funny and loved to chat about the past. Although we talked about Daddy when he was a boy, Uncle Harry never brought up Daddy the adult.

Then one afternoon he said, as casual as anything, "Your mother tells me you refuse to speak to Colin."

I felt betrayed. All of a sudden, Uncle Harry was criticizing my behavior. And I didn't like the idea that he and Mom discussed me, as if I had a problem that had to be handled with care.

Uncle Harry waited for my reaction, but I wouldn't give him the satisfaction of saying one word.

"Not that I can blame you," Uncle Harry finally said. "When Colin called and told me what he was planning to do, I blasted him. Told him not to be such a fool."

"You did?" I asked, surprised that Uncle Harry was on our side. After all, he was Daddy's relative.

"I had to. I'm your father's oldest living relative." Uncle Harry shook his head. "Of course it didn't do any good. He went ahead and married that young woman and moved all the way to Kentucky. People generally do what they want to do. There's no stopping them."

"And that's why I won't talk to him," I said, relieved that he understood. "I'm glad you agree with me."

"Well, I don't know about that," Uncle Harry said. "Your father's remarried, which makes it pretty much a permanent situation. The way I see it, now's the time for some rethinking."

"What do you mean?" I was hurt. I had thought that Uncle Harry understood how I felt, but now I wasn't sure.

"There's no point in cutting off your nose to spite your face. Don't you think having a long-distance father is better than not having a father at all?"

"He chose to leave," I said stubbornly.

"Indeed he did," Uncle Harry agreed. "And he did lots of other not-so-nice things, I gather. Still, he loves you." His voice sounded more casual, but I knew he was getting down to the point he wanted to make. "Anyway, I was thinking about *you*."

"What do you mean?" I asked suspiciously. He was beginning to sound a lot like Bobby.

"Well, I think you're doing your best to pretend you don't love him anymore, when you do. Very much."

"No, I don't," I contradicted him softly.

"I bet you'd love to talk to him, but you think it would be a sign of weakness if you were to pick up the phone and call him."

He was too near the truth for me to answer. Actually, I had thought of wishing Daddy a happy New Year. But by the time I could bring myself to tell Corrine, she had already hung up the phone.

"And I bet your father would love to hear from you," Uncle Harry went on in a low, insistent voice.

"Mmm," I said politely. "Do you think we could change the subject? It's getting boring."

"Whatever you like, Cassie," Uncle Harry said. He had a twinkle in his eye, so I knew he didn't think I was being disrespectful.

I thought about our conversation later that night when I was falling asleep. I wasn't ready to talk to Daddy. Not yet. Maybe I never would be.

CHAPTER 13

anuary turned into February. Soon it would be Valentine's Day. Not that *I* cared about Valentine's Day, but that was all Corinne talked about — every single day. After listening to Corinne, I was beginning to believe that Valentine's Day had changed from February fourteenth to February tenth. Because Saturday, February tenth, was the date of the Sweetheart Dance at Townsend High.

Of course Corinne was going with Jason, along with a group of their friends. Corinne was especially excited because her best friend, Leslie, was going to the dance with Jason's best friend, Ross. Leslie and Ross had suddenly discovered they liked each other one day in the student lounge. My sister took this to be a mystical sign that the four of them would always be friends and care about one another. Ick! It was nauseating how Corinne went on. She talked Mom into buying her a new outfit, and every day we had to hear about how great the dance was going to be. I knew Corinne was hoping Jason would give her a gift on Valentine's Day. A gold heart on a chain, to be exact.

"Really, Corinne, you're acting like this is a prom," I finally complained after she'd monopolized our Sunday dinner conversation trying to decide which earrings she should wear. "Or a wedding, at the very least."

Corinne waved her hand to dismiss me. "You're too young to appreciate the importance of details, Cassie. A mere eleven-year-old."

"I'll be twelve next month, and I'm old enough to know you're going soft in the head over this dumb dance."

Corinne didn't even bother to make her witch face at me. Maybe she was maturing, after all.

But all this excitement about the dance didn't stop her from arguing with Jason. Once it was because she wanted him to get a new blazer, and he refused to. Another time, I heard her say over the phone, "No, let's go in Ross's car. It's newer than yours, and roomier for six people."

I always had mixed reactions when Corinne treated him that way. I couldn't help feeling sorry for Jason, because he was a nice guy. But I was glad to see Corinne getting her way in a world where men had the upper hand.

The Friday before the dance, Corinne came home on the four o'clock bus and rushed into the house. I'd had just enough warning from Uncle Harry to gather up my stamps in time. I was sliding everything under my bed when she stomped into the bedroom.

"You were right, Cassie. I don't know how a little kid like you knew it, but you were right all along."

It was so amazing to hear Corinne say I was right about anything, I could only stare at her. Her eyes, which were ringed with mascara, had a wild look. And for once, her hair was a mess.

"Men, boys, they're all the same. You can't depend on them." She started to cry. "They always let you down at the worst possible moment."

"What happened?" I asked, a sinking feeling in my stomach.

"Jason broke up with me." Corinne was sobbing now. "He said he's been wanting to do it for weeks now, but he thought he could get through the dance for my sake. Only —" She had to gulp in air. "Only he says he can't continue this charade any longer. He took back his jacket, too-ooo."

I felt a terrible pang of sadness, as if Jason had left me, too. I guess I'd gotten used to having him around without even realizing it. "But he really likes you," I said stupidly.

"Oh, he likes me all right," Corinne said fiercely. "More than he's ever liked any other girl. But he says he can't put up with my bossiness. Can you believe that?" Corinne started to wail.

I didn't know what to say. Corinne *was* bossy with Jason, but I couldn't tell her that. I had to make her feel better, not worse.

"And the dance," she moaned. "I never looked forward to anything in my life as much as I looked forward to that dance. The new outfit. All those plans." She looked at me as if we'd changed ages. "How am I supposed to go on? I can't face everyone in school. They're probably all laughing at me."

Corinne buried her face in her pillow and sobbed. I didn't know what to do except put my hand on her heaving back. I wished there were some way I could take away the hurt and make Corinne as happy as she'd been all these weeks. That Jason! I gritted my teeth. If he were around, I'd punch him right in the stomach.

I looked at my sister lying there, crying softly into her pillow. Maybe she'll fall asleep, I thought. Maybe she'll feel better about things when she wakes up. And by that time, Mom will be home and know what to do.

I turned out the light and softly closed the door behind me.

I didn't want to be alone, so I went into the den where Uncle Harry was watching TV.

"Is Corinne all right?" he asked when I sat down on the couch. "She sounded upset, but I didn't want to intrude."

"Jason broke up with her."

Uncle Harry shook his head. "Poor girl. Still, I can't say I'm surprised, after the way she's been treating him."

"But Jason knows Corinne likes him," I insisted, defending my sister to the end.

"People like to be treated fairly. If they aren't, sometimes they get up and go."

"People get up and go, anyway," I said angrily, thinking of Daddy.

"Not everyone," Uncle Harry said mildly. "I stayed for thirty-seven years, and then your great-aunt Gertrude died." He gave a little chuckle. "In a sense, you could say she left me, now, couldn't you?"

I shrugged. My mind was on Corinne.

"I have an idea," Uncle Harry said. "Why don't you and I prepare dinner? Your mother left a chicken defrosting, which Corinne was supposed to roast. Gertrude had a wonderful recipe for chicken that was so simple, even I remember it. I believe your mom has all the necessary spices and everything else we'll need."

"Okay, Uncle Harry." He was right. We might as well keep busy.

We started the chicken and the rice, and I made a salad. Then I decided to check on Corinne. I opened the bedroom door and squinted into the darkened room. Corinne's bed was empty.

"Corinne," I called, thinking she might have gone into the bathroom. But when I looked, she wasn't there.

"Have you seen Corinne?" I asked Uncle Harry, who was busy putting some cooking utensils into the dishwasher.

"No," he said.

We searched the entire house, even the basement. Corinne was nowhere to be found. She'd left the house and we hadn't even heard her.

"Maybe she went to visit a friend," Uncle Harry suggested.

"I'll call Leslie," I said. But Corinne wasn't there. I told Leslie to call me the moment she arrived, knowing as I spoke that Corinne had no intention of visiting Leslie.

I looked into Uncle Harry's concerned face. I didn't want to upset him. After all, he was recovering from a heart attack. But this was a serious matter. Corinne was somewhere outside in the cold and the dark. We had to find her, and fast.

"I think we should get a taxi," I said, forcing myself to speak calmly.

Uncle Harry agreed. "Why don't you call one while I put on my shoes? Do you know where Jason lives?"

His question surprised me, though it shouldn't have. "I'm not sure, but he must be listed in Corinne's address book."

"Good. Bring the book. We'll go to Jason's first, then stop by all of her friends' houses."

"Okay. And I'm calling Mom." I felt a little better now that we had a plan.

We found Corinne in Jason's backyard. I got out of the cab and almost missed seeing her as she stood in the shadow of a huge pine tree. She was staring up at a lighted window on the second story that I knew must be Jason's room. And she wasn't even wearing her winter jacket, just a sweater and jeans. It reminded me of how I sometimes waited at Bobby's a moment after delivering the Schaeffers' paper, wondering what I would say if Bobby suddenly appeared. But of course it wasn't the same thing at all.

I went back to the cab and told Uncle Harry. "I'll go get her," he said softly. He jumped out of the taxi faster than I would have thought a seventy-five-year-old man could move. I watched him approach the still form of my sister. He took off his jacket and wrapped it around Corinne, then led her to the waiting cab. Corinne went willingly, as though she'd been waiting for someone to come and take care of her. Tell her what to do.

Mom was there when we got home. She put Corinne in a hot shower, then bundled her into bed and brought her something to eat. She stayed with Corinne for what seemed a very long time. Uncle Harry and I sat down to dinner, but neither of us ate very much. Mom finally came out of Corinne's room when Uncle Harry and I were doing the dishes.

"She's asleep," Mom told us with a little smile.

I took Mom's salad out of the refrigerator. "Mom, have

your salad while I heat up the rest of your dinner in the microwave."

Mom stroked my arm. "Thanks, honey, but I can't eat anything. Maybe later." She looked at Uncle Harry. "I should have realized Corinne was suppressing her reaction to the divorce, acting as though nothing were wrong. And now it's all compounded. She feels hurt and betrayed — by Colin *and* by Jason." Mom shook her head. "Poor thing. Now she has to deal with two losses instead of one."

"You mean the way she's been treating Jason has to do with Daddy's leaving?" I asked.

"I think so," Mom said. "I think she kept testing Jason to see how much he'd take because he liked her. And it blew up in her face. I tried to get Corinne to see the connection, but she can't — or she won't. She's feeling empty and worthless. She thinks all the kids in school are laughing at her."

"What can we do?" I was worried by what Mom had just said.

"Well, for one thing, I'm going to have her see that psychiatrist Jessie recommended. Dr. Shapiro worked wonders with the daughter of Jessie's friend."

"Do you think Dr. Shapiro will make her better?" I asked.

"I hope so," Mom said. She sighed. "Corinne will be all right. She just has to learn to deal with all her feelings." Mom looked meaningfully at me. "It's no use pretending we're not hurt when someone has upset our lives. Those feelings never go away. They can fester and harm us in different ways. Painful as it may be, we're better off dealing with them directly."

"Oh," I said, feeling uncomfortable. I was hoping Mom wasn't planning on having *me* talk to any psychiatrist. After all, I wasn't hiding anything, was I?

CHAPTER 14

The weekend seemed to stretch out forever. Corinne's friends kept calling on Saturday, but my sister wouldn't speak to anyone, not even to Leslie. Especially not to Leslie, who was going to the dance with Jason's best friend. Leslie was so upset, she told Mom she was going to break her date with Ross. Mom told her not to be silly, and to go ahead and have a good time.

Corinne stayed in bed, her face to the wall, dozing or listening to music. Mom brought Corinne's meals in on a tray. I asked if I could be there while she ate, but Mom shooed me away. She said Corinne wanted privacy. At night I tried to be as quiet as possible. Once I bumped into the wastepaper basket and made a racket. I was hoping that Corinne would get annoyed and yell at me for being clumsy. But she didn't say a word.

She'll get out of bed on Sunday, I told myself. Only she didn't. She lay there like a lump, with the radio turned down low.

"Corinne," I finally called to her in a loud whisper.

"Don't bother me, Cassie."

"Aren't you going to get up?"

"No. Go away."

I wondered if my sister was having a nervous break-down. Would she have to go to the hospital? My fear blazed into hatred toward Jason for doing this to my sister. But it wasn't Jason who was really responsible. It was Daddy. It was Daddy who had harmed Corinne by leaving us. I started hating him again.

Monday came, and Corinne refused to go to school. She stayed home Tuesday and Wednesday, too, moping around the house in her bathrobe, her face pale without its usual makeup, her hair as wild as a bird's nest. But mom made her get dressed on Thursday morning because they had an appointment with Dr. Shapiro.

I hurried home from school, eager to find out if the psychiatrist had helped her. I found Corinne straightening up her drawers, the CD player blasting old Beatles songs.

She's all right, I thought in amazement as I turned down the volume. Corinne made a face, but she didn't complain.

"I guess you saw the doctor today," I said.

"Uh-huh."

"And you're feeling better?"

"Absolutely. One visit and I'm all cured." Corinne laughed scornfully.

For the first time, she succeeded in making me feel like a two-year-old. Upset, I bit my lip. I'd never heard Corinne sound so bitter. I was foolish to think she was better just because she was doing her usual things.

"What was Dr. Shapiro like?" I asked, searching for something to say.

"She's okay. We talked for over an hour, and she said she wouldn't charge us overtime." Corinne glanced at me slyly. "She met Mom, and she wants to meet you, too."

"She does?" I gasped. "I mean, what for? I don't need a psychiatrist looking into *my* head."

Corinne laughed. "Don't worry, Cassie. She just wants to ask you some questions. Mostly about Daddy and the divorce."

"Well, I'm not going," I said heatedly, "and no one can make me. I mean, what's so great about this doctor? She can't even get you to go back to school," I said.

"That's how much you know," Corinne said loftily. "I'm going back to school tomorrow."

"You are?"

Corinne tossed back her hair. It was neatly arranged in its usual style. "I have to go back sometime, don't I?"

Impulsively, I threw my arms around Corinne and hugged her tight. "I'm glad you're all right," I said. "I — I mean, that you're acting like yourself. I was so worried about you."

Corinne hugged me back. "And you've been really good about everything. If you want, Tom can sleep in your bed."

"Great!" What was happening? I couldn't believe that one visit to a psychiatrist had suddenly turned Corinne into a generous person.

"Only on the condition that you stop complaining about my playing my music too loud." Corinne smiled. "Dr. Shapiro says everyone has to learn the art of fair negotiation."

So much for Corinne turning into a generous person. I'd have to stick cotton in my ears if I wanted to keep Tom in her room, but at least Corinne was going to be okay.

Corinne went back to school and seemed to adjust to life without Jason. I knew she still thought about him because sometimes she'd play "their songs" and her face would take on a sad, wistful expression. A few times, I overheard her talking to her friends about who Jason was dating. But she didn't carry on the way I was afraid she would, insisting that she couldn't live without him. I guess that was thanks to Dr. Shapiro.

Corinne saw the psychiatrist twice a week. Uncle Harry offered to pay but Mom said certainly not — it was Daddy's obligation to do that. And after a long discussion on the telephone, Mom hung up, her eyes shining with victory. "I got Colin to admit he's partly responsible for Corinne's state of mind," she told Uncle Harry.

So why were they both looking at me?

During the last week of February, it was my turn to see Dr. Shapiro. I didn't want to go, but Mom said it would be a one-shot deal. Just so that she could meet all of us — for Corinne's sake. Though I don't know what I expected Dr. Shapiro to look like, I was surprised to meet a plump, gray-haired woman with a jolly laugh, who could easily pass as someone's grandmother.

Dr. Shapiro smiled a lot. I knew she was trying to put me at ease, but her probing eyes, her questions, and her note-taking all made me very nervous. Was I saying the right thing? Was it what she wanted to hear? Or did she think I needed therapy, too?

I was about to jump out of my chair from all the tension when Dr. Shapiro stood and said our time was up. I let out a sigh of relief.

"Would you like to come and talk to me again?" she asked.

"No!" I answered, probably more loudly than was polite. Dr. Shapiro's eyes widened in surprise.

"I mean, I'm not like Corinne, am I?" I asked, the question just popping out.

"You are an intelligent preadolescent, Cassandra, with a strong sense of yourself. I doubt very much that what happened to Corinne will happen to you. You and your sister are two very different people. You're reacting to your parents' sudden divorce in different ways."

I smiled, glad to hear that. I mean, I knew I wasn't like Corinne, but it was good to hear a psychiatrist say so.

Dr. Shapiro continued, "However, in your own way, you are resisting the reality of the new situation. If you should ever decide that you want to come back and discuss your feelings about your father, simply tell your mother, and she'll arrange an appointment."

I mumbled a polite good-bye, then zipped through the door and into the waiting room at record speed. Mom looked up from her magazine and went in the office to have a few words with Dr. Shapiro. I ran out into the cold, crisp air. Maybe Corinne liked talking to a psychiatrist, but for me it was as bad as having to give a speech in front of the entire school.

I was glad when February was over and March began. Bobby always hated March because of the wind and the cold and the fact that some years there wasn't one single holiday in the entire month. But I loved March. For one thing, it was the month of my birthday. It was also the beginning of spring, and the best things — warm weather and summer camp — were yet to come.

Although sometimes it was so windy that the newspapers practically flew from my hands as I delivered them, the days were also growing longer and milder. Uncle Harry was feeling good. He'd walk into town whenever the weather allowed. I'd go with him when I could.

"I know I'm recovering faster than I would have if I'd stayed at home," he told me. "Older people thrive when they're surrounded by people they love."

"I'm glad you're feeling better, Uncle Harry," I told him, taking his hand. "And I'm glad you're with us, too." I didn't say so, but it was nice being a family again — with Uncle Harry instead of Daddy. Daddy. Ha! I hardly ever thought of *him* anymore.

I turned twelve on March eleventh. My birthday was on a Sunday. I invited Melissa and Janie to have dinner with Mom, Corinne, Uncle Harry, and me at my favorite Italian restaurant. Afterward, we went back to the house for birthday cake. My cake was shaped like a sleeping cat and had lemon filling — my favorite kind. Everyone sang "Happy Birthday" and I blew out the candles, wishing for a new bicycle. We ate, and of course I gave a piece of cake to Tom. Then I opened my presents. They were the best ever! A blouse and Capri pants from my friends; a flower pin from Corinne. Uncle Harry gave me an elegant gold bracelet with a small diamond in the middle. I found a plastic envelope inside his card. I knew it held stamps.

"Thanks, Uncle Harry," I said, throwing my arms around him. "I love what you bought me."

"At least I got it right this time," he said to Mom.

Mom, Corinne, and Uncle Harry laughed while I blushed, remembering the stuffed dog that I'd stuck somewhere in the basement. I opened Mom's card and was reading her note, which promised me a new bicycle as soon as I could go with her to pick it out, when the phone rang. Corinne went into the kitchen to answer it. She returned a minute later, a funny look on her face. "It's for you, Cassie. Someone wants to wish you a happy birthday."

I was so excited about my party, my gifts, and turning twelve that I didn't think to ask who was on the line.

"Hello?" I said.

"Hello, Cassie. It's Daddy. Happy birthday, honey."

Daddy! He sounded so familiar, yet unreal and far away, as though he were speaking to me from a dream. "Hello, Daddy. How are you?"

"I'm okay, Cassie. It's been a rough year, but I'm adjusting to my life here in Louisville."

I frowned. "I'm adjusting to my life, too, Daddy."

"I know it's been difficult for you," Daddy said quickly. "I hope you understand that I never meant to hurt you. I love you, Cassie. I think of you every day."

"I love you, too, Daddy. And I miss you." The words just spilled out.

"I'd like you to come and visit us in April, during your spring vacation. Corasue is looking forward to getting to know you and Corinne. We've furnished our spare room especially for you girls."

"I don't know," I said, feeling overwhelmed. "I have to think about it." It was like wading playfully at the shore, then suddenly having to retreat from a large wave that threatened to knock me down and make me sorry I'd ever stepped foot in the water.

"I didn't mean to rush you, honey. Did you get my birthday present yet?"

"No," I said.

"The mail must be slow. I sent you a check for a hundred dollars, to spend any way you like."

"Thanks, Daddy."

"You're welcome. Here's Corasue. She wants to wish you a happy birthday, too."

Corasue. In my mind, I saw Corinne looking up at Jason's window. I saw her lying in her darkened room, a blanket-covered lump facing the wall.

I hung up the phone.

Daddy called right back, but I wouldn't talk to him. I wrote him a note thanking him for the money, which came the next day. I also mentioned that I wouldn't be visiting him during spring vacation. What I *didn't* mention was that he shouldn't have tried to put Corasue on the line. Daddy should have been smart enough to know that speaking to him was more than enough for me to handle in one day.

I tried to remember how Daddy used to be. Had he really understood me all those years, or was that something I'd imagined? Could he have changed so much, or was I re-membering him all wrong? I thought and thought about it until my head began to ache. I felt confused. I was begin-ning to wonder if my father was ever as smart and as nice as my memories — which were beginning to fade.

CHAPTER 15

The week after my birthday, Mom announced she was throwing a cast party for the Red Barn Players. The members took turns hosting parties after the last performance of each play they performed. Saturday night marked the end of their four-week run of *The Middle of the Night* by Paddy Chayefsky. Mom wanted to give *this* party to celebrate her new position. Jeff and Nancy had just made her production manager of the company.

Mom bought all of the food and drinks and paper goods. She asked Corinne and me to do a few things like making the coffee and heating up the hors d'oeuvres and casseroles. The play ended around ten forty-five, which meant people would start arriving after eleven. I thought it was a dumb time to have a party, but I didn't say so. Mom looked so happy and proud of herself.

Another thing I couldn't understand was why Uncle Harry and Corinne were so interested in Mom's party. I suppose Uncle Harry was eager to talk to someone other than the three of us. And Corinne — it was the first time I'd seen her excited about anything since she and Jason broke up.

She chatted on in her silly way about how wonderful it was to meet people in the arts. As if the people who were coming to our house were real actors and actresses. It got on my nerves.

"Corinne, don't make such a big deal about the theater group," I said. "They're only teachers and accountants during the day, just like Mom's other friends." I couldn't help adding, "I mean, I *did* meet most of them at the New Year's Day party."

"Well, well," Corinne taunted. "Aren't we turning into a little Miss Know-It-All."

I flushed. I should have left out the bit about the party.

"Sure they have other jobs — so they can eat. Look how many actors in New York City are waiters and cab drivers," Corinne said, insisting on her dumb comparison.

I made a face, which she ignored.

"Besides," Corinne went on, "they must have *some* talent or their group wouldn't be so successful. Mom says the last few performances were sold out. In fact, they had to turn people away for the very first time."

"Part of that was Mom's doing," I reminded Corinne. "Remember how she insisted that they advertise in all the newspapers?"

Corinne nodded. After a minute, she said, "It's funny how Mom turned out to be good at running the theater group. She's always been so scatterbrained about getting things done around here."

"Yeah," I said harshly. "Too bad Daddy didn't know that about her. Maybe he would have stuck around if he did."

Corinne surprised me by putting her arm around me. "Well, I'm really proud of Mom."

"Me, too," I agreed.

*   *   *

The evening of the party, Uncle Harry treated us to a take-out Chinese dinner. Afterward, Mom got dressed while Corinne and I cleared the table. She came back to give us our last-minute instructions.

"Mom, you look so pretty," I told her. She was wearing a floral-patterned silk top over black stretch jeans and high-heeled strappy sandals. Her strawberry blond hair had been shaped and blow-dried that morning.

"Thanks, honey." Mom smiled at me. "I *feel* pretty." She got down to business. "Now, girls, remember to heat up the mini hot dogs and cheese puffs at eleven. Start the coffee then, too." Mom put her hands to her head. "Oh, and don't forget the casseroles or the ice."

"Don't worry, Mom," I said. "I have everything written down." I waved the paper in the air.

She looked from me to Corinne. "And you're sure that neither of you minds playing waitress tonight?"

"It'll be fun," Corinne said. "I just hope that Cassie doesn't fall asleep on her feet."

Mom gave me a worried look. "It is kind of late for you to stay up, Cassie."

I glared at my sister, who was up to her usual tricks. "Corinne likes to pretend that I'm a baby so she can feel important. I won't fall asleep, Mom, and everything will be set when you step through the door. I have the CDs you picked out, ready to be played."

Mom patted my arm. "You girls do have everything under control. I know I shouldn't worry, only — it's just —"

"That I'm *ner-vous!*" Corinne and I chorused. Mom laughed. It was natural that she felt a little scared. This was the first party she was hosting since Daddy had left us. Another first, although now it seemed as if Daddy had been gone for years.

We finally convinced Mom to leave for the theater. Corinne went into her room to decide what to wear to the party. I wandered into the den to watch TV with Uncle Harry. But I couldn't sit still. I kept getting up — for soda, for a cookie, or to bring in Tom from where he was resting on my bed.

"You have the worst case of ants in the pants that I've seen in a long time," Uncle Harry commented when I returned for the fifth time, munching a cracker.

"I feel so restless," I admitted. "I keep worrying I'll forget to do something important. Or that I'll start yawning — like Corinne said I will."

"Why don't you take a nap in your mom's room?" Uncle Harry said. He saw me consider the idea, then reject it. "Don't worry. I'll wake you up whenever you say."

"Okay. Make it ten o'clock." I grinned. "And please ask Corinne to lower her music. She'll listen to you."

I watched TV in Mom's room, doubtful that I'd fall asleep. But I must have, because the next thing I knew, Uncle Harry was tapping my shoulder and saying it was time to get up. I was glad I'd told him ten o'clock, because that gave me plenty of time to get dressed. I put on a long-sleeved red tee, my favorite jeans, and the platform clogs I never dared to wear outside. I brushed my hair and pulled it back with a scrunchy. Then I put on the gold bracelet from Uncle Harry and smiled at my image in the mirror.

Suddenly, I was in a party mood. I went into the den and put on a tape. It was Billy Joel, one of Mom's favorites. The music came on loud, filling the house. I didn't bother to turn it down.

"Oh, there you are, Cassie," Corinne said, walking in from the kitchen. She was wearing the outfit Mom had bought her for the Sweetheart Dance. She looked so lovely, I was speechless for a moment.

Corinne thought I was staring at her outfit for another reason. "I figured I might as well wear it," she said, a little embarrassed, "instead of letting it rot in my closet."

I was about to tell Corinne how pretty she looked, when Uncle Harry came out of my room in a sports jacket and a tie. He beamed at us.

"I have the two most beautiful nieces in the world," he told Corinne and me.

"And you look handsome, too, Uncle Harry," I said.

"Just let me straighten your tie," Corinne said. She started fixing it before he could say a word. Uncle Harry and I looked at each other and held back our laughter. When it came to clothing, my sister thought she was the world's expert.

All at once, we had so much to do and not enough time to do it in. I got out my list.

"Corinne, put the hors d'oeuvres and the casseroles in the oven. Don't forget to turn it on. Three hundred and twenty-five degrees. Uncle Harry, could you make some ice cubes and store them in the freezer? The plastic bags are in the bottom drawer next to the sink."

I started removing the cellophane from the paper plates and cups and setting them out on the dining room table.

"Who made you the boss of this operation?" Corinne asked as she carried things from the refrigerator to the oven.

"I'm more efficient than you are, and you know it," I told her as I suddenly remembered the coffee.

For once, Corinne didn't answer me back.

*   *   *

Soon Mom's guests arrived, all of them within a couple of minutes of one another. The house was filled with people laughing and talking. Mom hurried into the kitchen to take care of the food, leaving Corinne and me to deal with her guests' coats. We were as polite as any butler, folding them carefully over our arms until we got to Mom's bedroom. Then, giggling, we threw them down on the bed, making a small mountain of cloth and fur for Tom to sleep on.

"We have to get the hors d'oeuvres and pass them around," I hissed to Corinne when I spotted her getting into a conversation with Jeff. She gave me a dirty look but followed me into the kitchen. I transferred the mini hot dogs while Corinne worked on the cheese puffs. We carried the trays into the den, where most of the guests were sitting or standing in small groups. Uncle Harry was in his glory, serving drinks like a professional bartender.

I circled around a few times, smiling and answering questions, until all the hot dogs were gone. I brought the empty tray back to the kitchen and poured myself a soda. There was nothing more for me to do, so I wandered back into the living room. People had formed small groups and seemed to be having the time of their lives. Even Corinne, who was chatting with a handsome man at least ten years older than her. Jeff's nephew, I think he said he was.

I realized I was the only child at a party of adults. I felt like the baby that Corinne always said I was. She was almost sixteen and, for all her silliness, knew how to act grown-up when she wanted to. Even Uncle Harry was talking up a storm to some old guy. I sighed and decided I might as well go to bed. No one would miss me, that was for sure.

"Cassie, come here and meet some of my friends," Mom

called to me from the living room couch. Sam, who I'd met at the New Year's party, was there, as well as an elderly couple and a dramatic-looking woman in a black dress, wearing at least thirty bangle bracelets on her arm.

I went over to them. "You remember Sam," Mom said, smiling.

"Hi, Cassie." Sam waved his hand and smiled. He didn't look as intense as he'd appeared at the New Year's party. In fact, he seemed quite pleased with himself.

"This is Andy and Marcia Greene. Andy's just joined our group, and Marcia's considering," Mom continued. "And this is Yolanda. She teaches dramatics in the same school as Jeff."

"Hello, Cassie." Yolanda smiled, flicking back her dark hair and almost hitting Sam in the face with it.

I squeezed in between Mom and Marcia, and they continued their conversation about the evening's performance: how this performance was head and shoulders above all the others and how the audience was totally involved with the play, especially in the final scene. Yolanda took everyone's comments and translated them into complicated theatrical terms. I couldn't understand most of what she was saying. The two things I *did* pick up, though, were that Sam had a pretty big part in the play and that Yolanda was interested in Sam.

"Do you really think I was effective in the second act?" he asked, looking at Mom. "I was so afraid of overdoing it that I held back more than I should have."

"You were terrific," Yolanda said emphatically. "I think you've finally learned to relax during a performance." She put her braceleted hand on his, but he pulled it away absentmindedly. He was acting as if he hadn't even heard what she'd said. He was waiting for Mom to speak.

"Yolanda's right," Mom said. "It's amazing how much you've grown from the first performance to the last. Now you're projecting both your emotions and your voice."

A big grin spread over Sam's bony face, making him look handsome. "Thanks, Claudia. If you say so, it must be true."

The Greenes both added their compliments. Yolanda scowled. I'd just learned something important: Sam was smitten by Mom, and Yolanda didn't like it one bit.

After a while, Corinne and I helped Mom put the cold cuts and casseroles on the dining room table, and everyone got up to eat. Then it was time for coffee and dessert. Mom set out the delicious cakes she'd bought that afternoon, and I pigged out on the chocolate blackout cake and blueberry cheesecake. By that time, I was relaxed and chatting with practically everyone at the party. I was so busy talking, I almost forgot we were supposed to be helping Mom. This time Corinne reminded me to collect the used plates and cups. We cleaned up, both of us yawning. And suddenly, the party was over.

"Go to sleep, the two of you," Mom said, putting an arm around Corinne and me. "We'll clean up the rest in the morning."

"Sure, Mom," I said, kissing her. "Great party."

"And you were a wonderful help," Mom said. "I couldn't have done it without you."

We said our good nights and got into our pajamas.

"Good night, Cassie," Corinne said to me in the darkness.

"Good night," I told her, and nestled into my favorite position to get ready for sleep.

CHAPTER 16

I couldn't fall asleep. I found myself wondering if I'd put out enough cups for coffee and tea. Had I remembered the artificial sweetener? My brain didn't seem to realize that the party was over. I'd had a great time, even though the guests were all adults. Many of them complimented me, saying that I was such a big help and — I could hardly believe this! — I looked just like Mom. But what made me the proudest was hearing everyone praise Mom for all she'd done for the theater group. I smiled, thinking they should only know how she used to run our house. Actually, she still didn't call when something needed fixing. Now she left a note on the bulletin board, and Uncle Harry saw that it got done.

I decided I was thirsty. I tossed off the covers, glad to have an excuse to get out of bed. There was plenty of soda left, so I headed for the kitchen.

I hadn't taken two steps when I noticed a dim light coming from the front hall. Was Mom still cleaning up, or was there a burglar in the house? I almost called out but something stopped me. It was a good thing, too. I tiptoed forward and saw Mom and Sam. They were in a tight embrace — kissing.

I froze and covered my mouth so they couldn't hear my gasp of horror. There were muffled words. The front door opened. More muffled words and laughter; then the door closed. I scurried back to Corinne's room.

Mom and Sam! Before, when she was telling him how well he'd performed, I believed she was only trying to be nice. I hadn't even thought about Mom caring for a man since that night she'd gone out with Jeff and I'd hung my WOMEN ONLY sign. Too bad I hadn't put up the sign tonight!

But that was silly. No sign would keep Mom from liking a man and maybe marrying him. Would she marry Sam? The possibility made me shiver, as if someone had dropped an ice cube down my back.

"Corinne, wake up." I shook my sister's shoulder. "I have to talk to you."

"What's the matter? What's wrong?" Corinne asked, groggy with sleep. She sat up, her back against the wall. I climbed on the bed to sit beside her.

"I caught Mom kissing Sam," I said.

Corinne thought a minute. Then she smiled. "Sam's cute. Mom has good taste."

"Be serious, Corinne. He's got to be ten years younger than her. What if they get married?"

"Oh, Cassie," Corinne said, exasperated. "You're making a mountain out of a molehill. It's a party. They're probably just in a friendly mood. Mom's never even gone out on a date with Sam."

"But he likes her. I know he does," I said, remembering how he'd waited for Mom to give her opinion about his performance.

"All right, so Sam likes her," Corinne said firmly. "And from what you're telling me, Mom likes him, too."

Mom likes him, too. Corinne made it sound so logical, so ordinary. But it wasn't ordinary to find out your mother liked some guy. It was happening only because Daddy had divorced her and forced her to look for someone else. Someone who would hurt her all over again, and who Corinne and I would probably fight with all the time.

My old feelings of anger and hurt toward Daddy, toward all men, filled my heart. I couldn't speak.

"Don't cry, Cassie." Corinne sounded just like Mom. She even put her arm around me the way Mom did.

"I'm not crying," I said as I reached for a tissue.

"Look, Cassie, we have to face reality. Sooner or later, Mom's going to start dating. She probably hasn't all these months because she's always with the RBP people. They've been like a family to her."

I blew my nose. "Which means she's always with Sam," I pointed out.

"Right. Which means she may have liked him for quite a while but hasn't gone out with him yet. Because of you."

"Because of me?" I asked, surprised.

Corinne shrugged. "She probably didn't want to upset you. I mean, see how upset you are. And" — Corinne giggled — "look at what you did to Jeff. You know his cute nephew, Randy? The one I was talking to?"

I nodded.

"Well, Randy says Jeff's afraid of you."

I started giggling, too. Soon we were laughing so hard, my sides started to ache. "Uncle Harry," I said, pointing to the wall. "We'll wake him up." This sent us into another fit of giggles.

Finally, we calmed down. I felt better. Then Corinne turned to me. In the light coming in from the streetlamp, I could see her eyes glittering in the dark. "You won't do anything to upset Mom when she starts dating, will you?" she asked, suddenly serious.

I bit my lip. I knew at that moment, as sure as Corinne was my sister, that one day Mom *would* remarry. And there wasn't one thing I could do about it — except to make her unhappy.

"I won't put up any signs, if that's what you mean," I said grudgingly.

Corinne hugged me. "You're all right, Cassie," she said, laughing. "And you'll *be* all right," I heard her whisper, as though to herself. After a minute, she gave me a little push. "Now go to sleep. It's late."

I got into my bed and immediately fell asleep.

Mom started dating Sam the next day. During breakfast — brunch, actually, since it was so late — she mentioned that they were going to the movies. She waited warily for my reaction while Corinne's eyes bored into mine, willing me to behave.

"That's nice," I said as casually as I could manage. "What are you going to see?"

Mom smiled with relief. "Well, we're not sure yet. We have to check the paper to see what's playing. Neither of us has been to the movies lately."

Both Uncle Harry and Corinne gave me nods of approval. It was impossible to act up with the two of them monitoring my every move. Still, I couldn't resist asking Mom how old Sam was.

"Thirty-two," she answered, grinning. "I think I'll enjoy going out with a younger man."

"He's cute, Mom," Corinne said, while I counted on my fingers. The age difference wasn't as bad as I had thought.

I was even sociable when Sam came to pick Mom up. He looked handsome in his jeans, plaid shirt, and leather jacket. "Have a good time," I called out as he led Mom to his car.

"Thanks, we will." Sam waved and smiled. He was obviously happy to be taking Mom out. And there was nothing I could criticize him for — yet.

Monday afternoon, I delivered my newspapers. Then Uncle Harry and I walked into town. We went along at a leisurely pace, both of us thinking our own thoughts. It was a nice, breezy day. I noticed that crocuses were sprouting in some of our neighbors' flower beds.

The warm weather made me think of summer vacation and going to camp. Of course I wanted to go back, but Mom said she didn't know if I'd be able to this summer. It depended on Daddy and whether he could afford to send me. It wasn't fair! Too many things depended on Daddy even though he was far away and no longer part of my life.

It was amazing how I could forget about Daddy for practically an entire day at a time. Then something would remind me of him — a place we'd been to, something he'd said. I'd hear his laugh or the tone of his voice in my head, and I'd get an ache to see him, or at least to call and just say hello. Until I remembered why he was gone, and I'd push away my feelings and forget about him again. I was getting good at forgetting.

*   *   *

Uncle Harry and I had crossed to Main Street when Mrs. Schaeffer drove by with Bobby. She honked and gave me a big wave, which I returned. I was hoping Bobby would wave back, but he didn't. He acted the way he did in school — like I wasn't even there.

"Who's that?" Uncle Harry asked.

"Mrs. Schaeffer. A lady on my paper route."

"What a friendly person," Uncle Harry commented.

"Well, I used to be friends with her son Bobby," I explained, wondering why I was feeling uncomfortable.

"Oh, yes. I believe I met him once. He seemed like a nice young fellow. What happened, Cassie?"

I shrugged my shoulders. "We had a fight."

"Did you ever think of making up?"

"I guess," I surprised myself by saying. "I mean, I'm not mad at Bobby anymore, but I feel funny apologizing after all this time. Besides, I don't think he wants to be friends again."

"You'll never know until you try it," Uncle Harry said.

"I'll think about it," I said, then immediately put the subject of Bobby Schaeffer out of my mind.

Our first stop was the post office. I'd been in to see Mr. Guerney a few times since I went to Mr. Flores's store. He greeted me as an old friend.

"Cassie Landauer!" he called out when it was our turn at the window. "Buy any nice stamps lately?" Apparently, that struck him as hilariously funny, because he started to laugh. When he calmed down, he greeted Uncle Harry and asked how he could help him. Uncle Harry was mailing some large envelopes full of business papers. He also wanted a book of stamps. Mr. Guerney weighed the envelopes.

"And here's a book of pretty birds, Mr. Landauer. How is your collecting going, Cassie?"

"I'm still working on the packet I bought from Mr. Flores," I said. "I don't get that much time to spend on my album."

"Children are so busy these days," he said, shaking his head. Suddenly, his eyes lit up. "Say, are you going to the stamp show in Manhattan? It's this coming weekend. I wouldn't miss it for the world."

The stamp show. I'd almost forgotten about it. But there was no way I could get into Manhattan. Mom wouldn't let me go by myself, and I sure wasn't planning on sneaking off without telling her — not after what had happened when I went to Glen Haven.

We said good-bye to Mr. Guerney. My head was still filled with thoughts about the stamp show. It would have been an opportunity for me to see rare stamps. And it would have been exciting, with crowds of people from all over the country.

"Would you like to go to the stamp show?" Uncle Harry asked.

He spoke so casually and quietly — as if he were asking me if we should go to the shoemaker's or the hardware store — that I thought I was imagining his question.

"Of course I want to go! But how can I? Mom won't let me go into the city alone."

"What if I came with you?"

I grabbed his arm. "You mean you'd come in with me? On the train?"

"Cassie, my dear." Uncle Harry was grinning. "How would you like to go to the stamp show by limousine?"

 was so excited about going to the stamp show that I had little patience for the rest of our errands.

"Slow down, Cassie," Uncle Harry complained as I practically dragged him from the hardware store, where he'd just bought washers for our dripping bathroom faucets. "We're not running a race here."

"Sorry, Uncle Harry," I apologized. "I can't wait to call Melissa and Janie and tell them about going to the show in a limo."

I did exactly that the minute we walked into the house. They both thought it was fantastic, especially the part about the limousine. "You're so lucky to have a rich uncle who will take you anywhere you want to go." Janie sighed. "My father complains whenever he has to drive me to dancing school."

"Uncle Harry's an all-right guy," I agreed, remembering how angry I'd gotten three months ago because he was coming to stay with us. Now it seemed as though he'd been living with us forever.

I had a sudden longing to tell Bobby. He would have been happy, knowing how much going to the stamp show meant to me. He'd always been generous that way. I shook my head to get him out of my thoughts. Why was I thinking about Bobby Schaeffer? Probably only because we'd passed him earlier in town.

I hugged Mom and gave her the news as soon as she came through the front door. She and Uncle Harry exchanged glances, then they both nodded. It was like they were having an entire conversation — which I pretended not to see.

"That's nice of Uncle Harry," Mom said, speaking as if he weren't there. "But why the stamp show, Cassie? I didn't know you were interested in stamps."

I hesitated only a second. "I've been collecting for months now, Mom. That's why I went to Glen Haven that time."

"Oh." Mom still looked puzzled, probably wondering why she hadn't known about my stamp collecting before. So Uncle Harry *hadn't* told her. I reached back and squeezed his hand.

"Actually, I'm using Daddy's old album. Uncle Harry gave it to him when he was my age," I explained, no longer needing to keep it a secret. "I never threw it out."

"Oh, Cassie," Mom said, and put her arms around me.

I felt tears welling up — because of Mom's sympathy and because of the reason that I'd kept the album in the first place — but I forced myself to remain calm.

"That's why I kept my job delivering papers through the winter," I told her. "So I'd have money to buy stamps. I can't wait to get to that show and buy some beautiful stamps."

"Well, of course," Mom said. "And all this time you must have thought I'd be upset because you wanted to add stamps to your father's album." Mom smiled. "It's perfectly normal for you to have kept something of his," she said, kissing my cheek.

And suddenly, it *was* all right, even logical, that I'd kept Daddy's album and made it my own. Especially now that I knew it had been a gift from Uncle Harry. Uncle Harry, Daddy, me — the album linked us together. It helped me remember that Daddy was my father, even though he was no longer a part of my everyday life.

Then Corinne came home and asked why we were all standing in the hall hugging one another and looking goofy, as if we hadn't seen one another in ten years.

Saturday turned out to be a perfect spring day. I wanted to look particularly nice, so I asked Corinne if I could borrow a shirt of hers that I liked. "Yeah," she mumbled as she turned over and went back to sleep. I put on the pin Corinne had given me and my gold bracelet. After I fixed my hair the way Corinne did hers, I smiled at myself in the mirror. I thought I looked pretty good.

The shiny gray limo pulled into the driveway at exactly nine o'clock. The driver held open the back door while Uncle Harry and I climbed inside. We sped along the highway, arriving in Manhattan in record time.

The stamp show was held in the ballroom of a large hotel. I pretended not to notice people staring at us as we left the limo. Uncle Harry told the driver to come for us at twelve-thirty. I stepped into the room and was overwhelmed by the rows of tables that seemed to go on forever. So many collections! So many stamps! I didn't know which way to turn. I walked toward the left and was drawn to a beautiful display of stamps from Monaco.

"Oh, look, Uncle Harry!" I exclaimed. "They're lovely! I could use some stamps from Monaco."

"How much are they?" Uncle Harry asked the dealer.

I gasped when I heard the price. Uncle Harry started bargaining with the man. Suddenly, my sweet, kind uncle was transformed into a shrewd businessman. And to my great surprise, Uncle Harry succeeded in buying the stamps for much less money than the dealer had originally asked for. He paid for them and handed them to me triumphantly.

"Gee, thanks, Uncle Harry," I said. "I'm really impressed."

Uncle Harry laughed. I could see he was pleased. I was about to head off to another booth when he said, "Let's start at one end and go up and down each aisle. Otherwise, you'll get all confused."

We did as he suggested. As we browsed, I noticed other people were bargaining, too. I grew bolder and started asking questions about stamps that I liked. Most of them were too expensive for me. Then we came upon some African stamps that weren't too costly. I offered to buy them at a lower price, and the dealer came back with another number. I was bargaining! Minutes later, the stamps were mine for what Uncle Harry told me was an excellent price.

I noticed that many of the dealers sold catalogs. They listed all the stamps ever printed anywhere. I'd looked through them in the library.

"Wouldn't it be nice to have your own set of catalogs, Cassie?" Uncle Harry asked me.

"I guess," I replied. "But you can't have everything in life, can you?"

Uncle Harry gave me a funny look. "I suppose not, only I learned that lesson when I was considerably older than twelve."

We were turning the corner and walking up a new aisle when I caught sight of Mr. Flores at a table several feet away.

"Mr. Flores!" I called out, and made a dash toward his booth. I slowed down when I saw his awful assistant staring at me like I was some kind of crazy person. And I *was* being silly, imagining that Mr. Flores would remember me when I'd only gone to his store once a few months ago.

Still, I offered him my hand. "I'm Cassandra Landauer, Mr. Flores. I guess you don't remember me, but I bought some stamps from you in December — the day it snowed."

Mr. Flores's dark eyes studied me. Then he grinned, showing white, even teeth. "But of course I do. You bought a large packet of stamps." He snapped his fingers. "I remember telling you about this show. And here you are!"

And here I am, I thought, pleased with myself. I bought a few stamps from Mr. Flores that he said were a wonderful buy. Uncle Harry offered to pay for them, but I wouldn't let him. "Thank you, but no," I told him. "I have plenty of money, especially with my birthday gift from Daddy."

"Independent, aren't you?" he joked.

"Yes, I am," I said. "Not that I don't appreciate the stamps you bought me," I added quickly. The last thing I wanted to do was hurt Uncle Harry's feelings.

We said good-bye to Mr. Flores and continued along the aisle. We were little more than halfway through the show when Uncle Harry said we had to leave.

"But we're not finished," I said, disappointed.

"Oh, we'll come back," Uncle Harry assured me. "We're only stopping for lunch."

The limo took us to a very exclusive French restaurant, as cool and dark as a cave, where too many polite waiters hovered over us. Uncle Harry helped me with the menu. I decided to try frog's legs. Uncle Harry ordered plain broiled fish. "No butter or oil, please," he told the waiter.

"It must be annoying to have to watch everything you eat for the rest of your life," I said.

Uncle Harry laughed. "More than annoying, I can assure you. But well worth the price of living to enjoy other things."

"Like what?" I asked.

"Like being able to escort my favorite niece to a stamp show," he said.

"Oh, Uncle Harry," I said, but I was touched.

The frog's legs turned out to be better than I'd expected. Even the vegetables were delicious, and the chocolate mousse was out of this world. I felt a little groggy from so much food, and I almost fell asleep in the limo on our way back.

But I came to life immediately as I showed the guard my stamped hand and reentered the show. Now it was crowded and more difficult to reach each table.

"I never dreamed so many people collected stamps," I said. "And my problem is, I like practically everything I see."

The one thing I decided to do was to begin another album — stamps of famous people. Uncle Harry insisted on buying me the album and some stamps of past American presidents to start me off. How could I refuse? I felt like a princess in the middle of a fairy tale in which I could have anything I wanted. But it all came to a sudden end when Uncle Harry said it was three-thirty and we had to leave.

"Okay," I said reluctantly, because there were still a few booths I hadn't seen.

"First I have to see a man about some books," Uncle Harry said. He told me to wait for him at the entrance to the show.

He returned a few minutes later, followed by a man with a carton on a small dolly. "What's this?" I asked.

"You'll see," Uncle Harry said.

The man followed us outside to where our driver was waiting. As we watched the man load the carton into the trunk, I said, "It's the catalogs, isn't it, Uncle Harry?"

"You're quick, Cassie," Uncle Harry said, and smiled.

"But it's too much," I protested. "Just bringing me here today was more than enough. Besides, you took me to that wonderful restaurant and bought me stamps and an album. And now these catalogs."

Uncle Harry could see that I was distressed. "Let's talk about this on the way."

The driver started for home. Uncle Harry took my hand in his. "Try to understand that it's my pleasure to give you the catalogs, Cassie, for all the wonderful time we've spent together. I can't tell you how happy you've made me. I never had a daughter, but if I had, I couldn't be more proud than if she'd turned out exactly like you."

My stomach was turning itself into a fist, the way it did when we had to give oral reports in front of the class and my turn was next. Uncle Harry was about to tell me something. Something I didn't want to hear. Something a lot more important than a set of catalogs or our trip into the city, which had been so perfect until now.

It came to me, and I shook my head no.

Today was Uncle Harry's way of saying good-bye.

CHAPTER 18

Y ou're going away," I said accusingly.

Uncle Harry nodded. "I was about to tell you when you beat me to the punch."

"But *why*, Uncle Harry?" I heard myself pleading. "I thought you were happy living with us."

"Indeed I am. Haven't felt so cared for since your great-aunt Gertrude died." He smiled sadly. "But it's time I returned to Philadelphia."

I gulped, afraid to ask my next question. "When are you leaving?"

"Next Sunday, I'm afraid."

"Next Sunday! That's so soon," I exclaimed. "Can't you postpone it for a while? Even for a week?"

Uncle Harry turned up his palms. "I'd love to, but it's impossible."

We rode in silence, my mind spinning as quickly as the four wheels beneath us. Uncle Harry had deceived me! All this time he'd been pretending that everything was fine, everything was normal, when all along he was planning his move back to Philadelphia. He knew it when he'd invited me to the stamp show. When he took me to the French restaurant and got me the catalogs. He was buying me off. Treating his fatherless grand-niece to the best day of her life so — his act of charity done — he could forget her as soon as he got home.

I crossed my arms and clamped my mouth shut to prevent another sniveling, begging word from escaping. If Uncle Harry wanted to leave us, let him! The sooner the better. I couldn't *wait* to have my bedroom back.

Uncle Harry tried to take my hand, but I pulled it away. He sighed. "Cassie, you're making this very difficult. I've my house and my business affairs to see to, and I can't put this off any longer." He smiled. "Also, now that I'm feeling so well, I have no right to impose on your mother's kind hospitality."

"I think it's unfair. How can you just go away and forget all about me?"

"I'll never forget you, Cassie," Uncle Harry said. "You've grown very dear to me these past few months. We'll call each other, and you'll come and visit me. Philadelphia's not that far away."

Why did those words sound so familiar? Where had I heard them before? Suddenly, I was blazing with anger, like a fire out of control.

"You're just like Daddy!" I yelled. "Like every man in this universe. You make someone care about you, and then you go away. And you talk about visiting, as if that's supposed to make everything all right."

Uncle Harry looked at me in astonishment. "Cassie, Cassie. How can you put my going home in the same category as what your father did?"

"But it feels the same," I said softly. "Like being left behind because you did something wrong, only you can't remember what it was — or why it was wrong."

Although I bit my lips to keep from crying, I couldn't stop the tears from rolling down my cheeks. This time I let Uncle Harry take me in his arms. They were frail and bony arms, but they comforted me as best they could. As much as anything could in my life, where nothing — and no one — seemed to stay forever.

Finally, I stopped crying. I sat up and sniffed until Uncle Harry offered me his handkerchief. I blew my nose and felt a little better.

"Cassie, try to realize that you didn't do anything to drive your father away," Uncle Harry said, as if we'd been talking about Daddy all along.

"But I feel like I did," I mumbled.

"Then maybe you'd better speak to that Dr. Shapiro," Uncle Harry said, "because you had nothing to do with Colin's going off with Corasue."

"And I couldn't have stopped him if I'd known about it — earlier?" I spoke so softly, I wasn't sure if Uncle Harry heard.

"No, you couldn't have," he answered firmly. "No one could. Not even your mother."

I felt relieved yet disappointed at the same time. After a while, Uncle Harry spoke.

"You knew I'd be going home eventually." He tapped his chest. "After all, I'm only seventy-five. There are some good years left in me still."

"I — I just didn't want to think about it," I admitted.

"You didn't want to think about it, but you were all ready to wash your hands of me, weren't you?" he asked with a chuckle.

"Well, I . . ." I suddenly felt embarrassed.

Uncle Harry took my hand in his. "Cassie, just because people don't live in the same house doesn't mean they stop loving each other. I meant what I said about having you visit me. I've hired a full-time housekeeper. She'll have a room ready for you anytime you like."

"Hmm," I said. I didn't want Uncle Harry to think he'd won me over that easily, but my mind was busy working. I could take the train or a bus to Philadelphia. Or maybe Mom could drive me there on a weekend when there wasn't a performance.

"What's Philadelphia like?" I asked.

"Oh, it's a great city," Uncle Harry said. "There's the Liberty Bell to see, and the place where they signed the Declaration of Independence. And young people gravitate to South Street, with its interesting stores."

"It sounds nice," I agreed.

"That's the advantage of having relatives in different parts of the country." He gave me a sly look. "You might even decide to visit Louisville one of these days."

Uncle Harry's last week zipped by, the way good times always do. I knew I'd miss him terribly, but I wasn't upset about his leaving, as I'd been the afternoon of the stamp show. Our talk in the limousine made me realize that he wasn't deserting me like Daddy. Uncle Harry simply wanted to go home. I couldn't stay angry with him for *that*. Besides, he really wanted me to visit — he wasn't just being polite.

Each afternoon, we walked into town, talking every step of the way. We planned what we'd do during my visit to Philadelphia over Memorial Day weekend. We discussed camp, which Uncle Harry said he'd pay for if Daddy couldn't. He even offered to pay for me to see Dr. Shapiro again. He explained that Dr. Shapiro wouldn't try to change my feelings toward Daddy, just help me understand what I was going through. I thought about all she'd done for Corinne, and I told Uncle Harry that maybe I'd go once or twice if it would make him happy. "Very happy," Uncle Harry said, and changed the subject.

I was glad Uncle Harry didn't think that Mom would marry Sam. Not that I didn't like Sam — I just didn't want any more changes in my life. The only person we didn't talk about was Daddy. Probably because Uncle Harry knew how it upset me to hear Corinne talk about visiting Daddy and Corasue during spring vacation.

"Sure you won't change your mind about coming?" she asked me.

"No," I snapped at her. "Now stop bothering me."

The truth was, I didn't *know* if I was going. Part of me wanted to see Daddy, to run into his arms. But part of me could never forgive him for what he'd done. Never in a million years.

I thought about Daddy whenever I was alone. I'd gotten so angry at him that I'd decided all males were the same. But they weren't the same. Uncle Harry wasn't like Daddy, and neither was Bobby. Sometimes Daddy wasn't even like Daddy. That was where I got confused — trying to understand how a person could love you yet desert you for someone else. I wanted to scream at Daddy, let him know how badly I hurt. Maybe I would go with Corinne to Louisville, after all. Just so I could tell him what was on my mind.

Mom made a special dinner for Uncle Harry the night before he left. Of course Uncle Harry wanted to take us all out to eat, but Mom said no — he'd done more than enough for our family. I asked Mom if we'd be able to manage money-wise without Uncle Harry's contribution. Mom laughed and said not to worry. We'd be fine, especially with her new raise.

Uncle Harry went back to Philadelphia the same way he arrived — by limousine. The driver who had taken us to the stamp show came for him on Sunday afternoon at one o'clock. He loaded Uncle Harry's luggage into the trunk. Uncle Harry kissed us all good-bye. I told him I'd call him that evening to make sure he had settled in all right.

Mom and Corinne went off in different directions, and I spent the afternoon putting my stuff back into my room. My room seemed familiar and strange at the same time. It still smelled of Uncle Harry's aftershave lotion. Tom wandered in and plopped himself down on the bed.

"It's our room again, Tom," I said as I stroked his back. He started purring, curled into a ball, and went to sleep.

The house seemed huge and empty without Uncle Harry. I went into the den and turned on the TV. Then I switched it off and wandered into the kitchen. I was too restless to work on my stamp albums. Melissa and Janie were at the movies. I wished I had someplace to go.

I wondered what Bobby was doing.

I was glad to get to school on Monday and be with my friends and classmates. Now that we were nearing the end of the year, school held the excitement of a series of parties. There was so much to look forward to: spring vacation, the Washington trip, the play, the dance, and, best of all, gradu-ation. It meant the end of elementary school—another end-ing. But there wasn't much time to feel sad.

During lunch, all Melissa and Janie could talk about was the yearbook.

"The candid shots came out great," Janie exclaimed as she twisted the end of her ponytail. "There's a great one of you in the library, Cassie."

"We're working on the yearbook dummy this week — setting up the pages for the printers to follow," Melissa told me. "The way that group likes to gab, we'll be up every night till midnight."

Melissa made a face as if she dreaded putting the dummy together, but I knew she was looking forward to it. I imagined six or seven kids sitting around Melissa's kitchen table, talking and laughing as they cut and pasted. Suddenly, I yearned to be a part of it all.

"Can I come and help?" I asked.

"I don't know, Cassie," Melissa said doubtfully. "Lots of kids asked to help put the yearbook together, but I had to tell them no because they weren't on the committee from the beginning."

"It's okay," I said quickly. "I understand."

"If you want to do something, there's always the school play," Janie said. "We're all trying out for that, aren't we?"

"Not me," I said. "I get nervous when I have to talk on-stage."

"Then work on the crew behind the scenes," Melissa said.

I remembered that Bobby was planning to do just that. Would he work with me? I realized I wanted that more than anything. But I wasn't sure I could make things right between us.

CHAPTER 19

I came home from school and had some cookies and milk, then set out on my paper route. The weather had turned blustery, and I wanted to finish up before it started to rain. Still, I took my time. The afternoon stretched ahead of me like the prairie in a book I was reading — flat and practically endless, with not much in sight.

Melissa and Janie were working on the yearbook, and Uncle Harry wasn't there to ask me how my day had been. I brightened up a little at the thought of calling him after dinner. When I spoke to him the night before, he said his house seemed so quiet after living with three women that he was considering getting himself a bird.

At Bobby's house, I put the newspaper by the door as usual. Then I found myself standing there, wondering if anyone was home. I couldn't hear anything, but that didn't mean much. I took a deep breath and rang the doorbell.

Nobody came to the door, so I rang again. Nothing. No one was home. I swallowed my disappointment. Well, at least I didn't have to face rejection, I told myself. After all, how did I know that Bobby would want to be my friend again? I'd been nasty and bad-tempered and, oh, so wrong. Besides, if he'd wanted to make up, there had been plenty of opportunities. Not a school day went by that we didn't pass each other in the hall.

I walked slowly toward my bicycle. Why bother rushing? I had only five more papers to deliver and nowhere to go but home. Even the thought of working on my stamp albums didn't excite me the way it had when Uncle Harry was around. It was funny how collecting stamps made me think of Uncle Harry now instead of Daddy.

"Cassie."

I heard my name in what I was sure was my imagination, so I kept on walking.

"Cassie," I heard again, this time louder, the voice closer. I stopped and turned around to wait for Bobby to catch up.

"Did you just ring the doorbell?" he asked, out of breath.

"Yeah, I guess."

"I was up in my room with the radio playing, so I wasn't sure if I'd heard the bell. I looked out and saw you walking away."

Bobby and I seemed to have run out of words. We looked at each other and down at the walk. I noticed that one of his sneakers was untied.

We spoke at the same time. "I was going to —" I began as he asked me if I wanted to come inside.

We laughed self-consciously. Then we looked at each other and really laughed.

I needed to apologize then and there, but it was hard finding the right words. "Sorry," was what you said when you bumped into someone, or when you forgot to make your bed after your mom especially asked you to because

133

company was coming. It didn't begin to make up for the way I'd treated Bobby.

"Bobby," I began, not sure of what I was about to say, "I want us to be friends again. I know it's my fault we're not talking," I said quickly, to get it all out, "and I know I have this terrible temper, but I'll try not to get angry ever again and — I'm sorry." There it was. That dumb expression. It sneaked in because no other was as good.

Bobby's answer was to grin and stick out his right hand. "Fine with me, Cass. Let's shake on it."

I grabbed his hand and pumped it up and down until he complained, "Hey, Cass, that's enough."

We went inside. Bobby showed me his new chemistry set and some other things he'd gotten since we'd stopped being friends. But mostly we talked. I told him about Corinne and Jason, about Mom's new job and her going out with Sam. About Uncle Harry and our trip into the city.

"What about your dad?" he asked when I got through. "You must have spoken to him by now."

"Once," I admitted, "on my birthday. But I hung up because he was about to put Corasue on the line."

"Cassie!" Bobby shook his head. "You'll have to see him one of these days."

"I guess. That doesn't mean I'll ever forgive him for what he did to Mom and Corinne and me."

"I can't blame you," Bobby said. He stared at me while a slow grin spread across his face. "Boy, I'm glad we're friends again. The drama coach asked me to be production manager of the play, and I sure could use your help. What do you say, Cass?"

"Great! I want to be involved in the play, but I hate getting up on stage."

"Fine, that's settled."

We went into the kitchen and had chocolate milk and cookies. We ate in silence, our words all spoken for now. Then a thought entered my mind. I tried to ignore it, but it loomed larger and larger, filling my head like a large balloon. I cleared my throat.

"Bobby, you're not planning to move, are you?"

Bobby thought a minute. He shook his head. "Nope. At least, no one's told me we are."

"You're *sure* that you're not going to move away without telling me about it?"

Bobby sighed with exasperation. "Of course not, Cassie. Why do you keep asking me that?"

"I don't know. With so many people leaving, I just wanted to make sure that you weren't, that's all."

I shrugged my shoulders to make it seem that it didn't really matter how he answered. But Bobby knew. Bobby always knew.

"Look," he said. "No one's said anything about leaving, but if my parents *do* decide to move, I promise to tell you. And" — he held up a finger because my mouth was opening to speak — "you couldn't blame me or get mad at me for that because it wouldn't be my fault."

"Okay," I meekly agreed.

Bobby wasn't finished. "And you can't get mad at me for being a boy, either. That's what I am, Cassie — a boy, who happens to be your best friend."

"I know, Bobby, and I'm glad." I grinned. Then I got up to go, and Bobby walked me to the door. It was like old times.

I hummed as I tore down the basement steps and into the storage room. The stuffed dog Uncle Harry had given me was lying facedown on top of the bureau. I petted its curly black head and long, floppy ears and took it upstairs to my room. Tom was on the bed, sleeping.

"Tom, this is Binky," I said, putting the dog on my pillow. "Now be nice to him because you two are going to see lots of each other."

Tom yawned and went back to sleep. I started humming again as I sat down at my desk and got out my stationery. "Dear Daddy," I wrote.

> I hope everything's good with you. We're all fine. Uncle Harry has gone back to his house in Philadelphia, but I plan to visit him. You know that old stamp album you had — the one Uncle Harry got for you? I thought you'd like to know I've been working on it.
>
> I won't be coming to visit you and Corasue during spring vacation. But I hope you can come up for my graduation. Without Corasue, please. I'm not trying to be difficult and I know I'll have to get to know her since she's my —

I gritted my teeth as I wrote

> — stepmother, but I really have to see you alone first so we can have that talk we never had. Please call and tell me if you can come or not.

I bit on the end of the pen as I thought about my next word, took a deep breath and wrote — "Love, Cassie."

I folded the letter and got it ready to mail. I wanted to send it out right away.

As I walked down the street, I thought of all the endings the past year had brought — the end of my parents' marriage, of Uncle Harry's visit, of elementary school. But I felt a twinge of excitement as I slipped my letter into the mailbox. I was ready for new beginnings.

About the Author

Marilyn Levinson taught Spanish for many years before returning to her first love, that of writing fiction. She is the author of many well-received novels for children, among them *Rufus and Magic Run Amok*, a Children's Book Council/International Reading Association selection as one of their "Children's Choices for 2002."